WEST

Jean Muir's job as house surgeon in the Trauma Unit at Westhampton Royal is gruelling enough, even without the difficult and demanding ways of her new chief Alex Mackenzie—and the bitchiness of his girlfriend Pauline is just the last straw! So how on earth does she find herself falling in love with him?

*Books you will enjoy*
*in our Doctor–Nurse series:*

AUSTRIAN INTERLUDE by Lee Stafford
SECOND CHANCE AT LOVE by Zara Holman
TRIO OF DOCTORS by Lindsay Hicks
CASSANDRA BY CHANCE by Betty Neels
SURGEON IN DANGER by Kate Ashton
VENETIAN DOCTOR by Elspeth O'Brien
IN THE NAME OF LOVE by Hazel Fisher
DEAR DOCTOR MARCUS by Barbara Perkins
RAINBOW SUMMER by Sarah Franklin
SOLO SURGEON by Lynne Collins
NEW DOCTOR AT THE BORONIA by Lilian Darcy
HEALERS OF THE NIGHT by Anne Vinton
THE RETURN OF DR BORIS by Lisa Cooper
DOCTOR IN NEW GUINEA by Dana James
PARIS NURSE by Margaret Barker
ROSES FOR CHRISTMAS by Betty Neels
NURSE IN BERMUDA by Helen Upshall
YESTERDAY'S LOVE by Judith Worthy
NURSE BRYONY by Rhona Trezise
THE FAITHFUL FAILURE by Kate Norway
SURGEON ON SKORA by Lynne Collins
THE CRY OF THE SWAN by Sarah Franklin
NOT AGAIN, NURSE! by Leonie Craig

# WESTHAMPTON ROYAL

BY

SHEILA DOUGLAS

MILLS & BOON LIMITED
London · Sydney · Toronto

*First published in Great Britain 1975*
*by Mills & Boon Limited, 15–16 Brook's Mews,*
*London W1A 1DR*
*This edition 1984*

© Sheila Douglas 1975

*Australian copyright 1984*
*Philippine copyright 1984*

*ISBN* 0 263 74573 2

*All the characters in this book have no existence outside the imagination of the Author, and have no relation whatsoever to anyone bearing the same name or names. They are not even distantly inspired by any individual known or unknown to the Author, and all the incidents are pure invention.*

*The text of this publication or any part thereof may not be reproduced or transmitted in any form or by any means, electronic or mechanical, including photocopying, recording, storage in an information retrieval system, or otherwise, without the written permission of the publisher.*

*This book is sold subject to the condition that it shall not, by way of trade or otherwise, be lent, resold, hired out or otherwise circulated without the prior consent of the publisher in any form of binding or cover other than that in which it is published and without a similar condition including this condition being imposed on the subsequent purchaser.*

Set in 10 on 11 pt Plantin
03/0284

*Made and printed in Great Britain by*
*Richard Clay (The Chaucer Press) Ltd*
*Bungay, Suffolk*

## CHAPTER ONE

Jean Muir drove through the main gates of Westhampton Royal Infirmary. She was glad that her journey was over because she disliked motorway driving, especially at night.

She turned left into the parking area reserved for the staff. At this late hour most of the cars there belonged to young resident doctors like herself. She locked up a little clumsily because she was tired, and picking up her small case made for the main entrance.

In the distance, outside the ever-open doors of the Accident Department, a couple of ambulances were parked. Jean glanced at her watch. Midnight, but that made no difference to the Accident Department, which was open twenty-four hours a day.

Westhampton was a large industrial town in the Midlands. Many of the factories worked night shifts, so the Accident staff could on occasion be as busy at three in the morning as at three in the afternoon.

Jean pushed against the heavy swing doors, and raised a hand in greeting to the two men in the porters' lodge.

'Evening, Dr Muir,' one called.

'Been off for the weekend?' the other asked.

Jean smiled and nodded, and turned off the main hall in the direction of the residents' quarters. She went through the door marked 'Private. Resident Medical Staff', and into the common-room, which was empty.

Someone had left the television on, and the room had the usual look of chaos about it. Jean, a tidy girl, turned off the television, cast a disapproving look around and decided to go in search of a much-needed cup of tea. The doctors had their own kitchen, but it was the custom for them to meet in the Night Superintendent's office, when they had done their late ward rounds.

Westhampton Royal was a friendly hospital, with excellent relations between nursing staff and doctors. That was why Jean loved it so much, in spite of the fact that her post as House Surgeon to the Trauma Unit was one of the most gruelling jobs there.

Two Night Sisters and several young doctors sat around drinking tea in the big outer room. The Night Superintendent herself was at her desk in the small inner office, where all the serious work was done. Everyone greeted Jean and one of the Night Sisters poured her a cup of tea.

'Evening, Dr Muir. Been home for the weekend?'

Jean nodded. 'Yes, and each time I go I think I'm an idiot not to take the train. How I hate motorway driving!'

'Pity we're never free the same weekends or you could come with me. I usually go to London.'

That was Tony Wilson, one of the registrars on the Trauma Unit, a good-looking young man with a roving eye. Jean didn't entirely approve of him, but like everyone else found it difficult to resist his charm. She wondered if he had a girl-friend in London. Several, probably, knowing Tony.

'Have you heard the news, Dr Muir?' asked the junior Night Sister, Liz Davies. She and Jean had become very friendly lately, but on duty it was always 'Doctor' and 'Sister' for the sake of discipline.

'What news?' Jean asked, so they all started to explain.

'Sir Geoffrey's had a coronary.'

'He's in the Intensive Care Unit.'

'It happened Saturday morning.'

Sir Geoffrey was Jean's chief, the Senior Surgeon on the Trauma Unit.

'He should never have come back to work,' Tony said. 'A two-week locum would have been O.K., but a long spell on our unit is too much for a man of sixty-seven.'

Sir Geoffrey, who had retired most unwillingly two years

ago, had leapt at the chance of coming back to his old job. The chance had been available because Mr Mackenzie, who had replaced Sir Geoffrey, had gone to the States for a six months post-graduate course that was something to do with the World Health Organisation.

'How bad is he?' Jean asked anxiously, because she was genuinely fond of the old man, who had been very kind to her during her first nerve-racking days in the operating theatre.

'Pretty bad,' Tony said soberly. 'But there's more to come. Alexander Mackenzie is flying back tomorrow, so from now on, my girl, we'll all have to be on our toes.'

Mr Mackenzie had a reputation for being difficult, tough on his juniors and a dynamo for work. During the six months Jean had spent at the Royal when she was working as a house physician, she had seen him sometimes in the distance, a tall man who walked faster than anyone else, so that his colleagues found it hard to keep up with him.

'Surely they could have found another locum consultant?' she asked. 'He can't have wanted to leave in the middle of his course.'

'The hospital secretary was on the telephone all Saturday,' Tony told her. 'There isn't a senior locum to be had at such short notice. So of course he would come back, wouldn't he? It is his Unit, after all.'

'Half his Unit,' Jean murmured, wishing that she worked for the other Trauma surgeon, a courteous and considerate man, who might not be as brilliant as Mr Mackenzie, but was certainly more easy-going.

'Don't look so alarmed,' Liz Davies said. 'He's not as bad as his reputation. I like the man myself.'

Liz was a hundred per cent efficient, highly intelligent and afraid of nobody. Jean sighed, wishing that she had the same approach to life.

'I only took the job because Sir Geoffrey was the chief,' she said. 'He sort of talked me into it, when I didn't get that job in General Surgery.'

'And to think that you could have had a cushy post on the Plastic Surgery Unit at your father's hospital,' Tony teased her. 'If I had a father who was a professor at a teaching hospital I should take advantage of it. What a funny girl you are, Jean!'

'Not funny,' Jean demurred. 'I just like being independent.'

Her family had said almost the same as Tony, when she didn't apply for a post at the hospital where she had been trained, and where several generations of her family had held senior appointments.

'I don't understand you, Jean, going to work in a horrible industrial town where you know nobody.' Those were her father's words, and when at the end of her six months in medicine, she had signed on for a further six months as a house surgeon, her mother had been even more outspoken.

'Anyone would think you were trying to get away from us, darling.'

It had been impossible to explain her reasons, because loving her family, she didn't want to hurt them. However, her mother had been uncomfortably near the mark. She did want to get away from them, for a time at any rate.

Jean was the youngest child of a brilliant family, an only girl with four older brothers, who alternately bullied and spoilt her, and seemed reluctant to admit that she had grown up. Her parents were just as bad, and after twenty-three years as the baby of the family, Jean had felt the need to strike out on her own.

Later, looking out of her bedroom window over the moonlit roofs of Westhampton, she recalled a conversation she had had this very weekend.

'Why do you keep on about its being a horrible industrial town?' she had asked crossly. 'It's a place where a quarter of a million people live and work and get ill, and finally die. Someone has to work in places like that, after all.'

Her brother Tom had clapped this unusually impassioned outburst of his sister's ironically.

'My word! A girl with a mission in life! I never knew little Jean had it in her.'

Tom was the cleverest of them all and worked in the field of computer medicine. He was also the next in age to Jean, and had perhaps resented being supplanted as the youngest. So there had always been a rather stormy relationship between them, which had increased now that Jean was old enough to understand what made her clever brother tick.

Resentfully she had countered Tom's jibe. 'At least I do care about people. All you're interested in is feeding facts into your beastly computers—and your own career, of course.'

Tom had flushed angrily, but before a full-scale family row could blow up, their father had interposed.

'Jean's right, Tom. Someone does have to do the donkey work in medicine. Our high-powered research in the top hospitals wouldn't be much use without all the dedicated men and women in the rest of the country.'

On Monday morning there was a nine o'clock operating list, so Jean was down early to breakfast. Tony Wilson was already there, talking to the Senior Registrar on the Trauma Unit, Mr Pollock. It was obvious that they were discussing the return of Alexander Mackenzie, and Pollock at any rate was decidedly lacking in enthusiasm.

'I shall miss the old man. It's been marvellous having him back this last two months.'

Pollock, Jean knew, had been six years a senior registrar, so had worked for a long time with Sir Geoffrey before he retired.

'When is Mr Mackenzie arriving?' she asked, and Pollock said rather sourly, 'He flies back today, and will be starting work tomorrow. You would think he could have left us to cope for a week or two on our own, but apparently he doesn't trust us.' He pushed back his chair and stood up. 'Don't be late in Theatre, Miss Muir. I'll be starting in five minutes.'

When he had gone Jean lowered her voice so that the other residents shouldn't hear what she asked Tony.

'Does Pollock dislike Mackenzie?'

Tony shrugged. 'Envies him, I suppose. They're much of an age, and yet here's Mackenzie a consultant while poor old Pollock is still only a registrar. And to make it worse Pollock was one of the unsuccessful candidates when Mackenzie got this job.'

'I didn't know that. Surely it would have been easier for Pollock—less embarrassing, I mean—to look for something else?'

Tony laughed. 'Senior registrarships don't grow on trees! We don't all have influential relatives to smooth our way, you know.'

Operating that Monday turned out to be heavy going. It was an all-day list, with two theatres working, Pollock in one, and Tony doing the less important cases in the other.

Pollock, who was usually easy on Jean, snapped at her several times. The weather was unusually hot for May and Jean, sweltering inside her theatre clothes, was heartily glad when they finished. She was writing up the operation notes on the last patient when Pollock came up to her, tugging off his mask and wiping the sweat from his face with it.

He looked tired and older than usual. 'I know it's been a tough day,' he said, 'but I want to do a ward round after tea.'

This wasn't the routine on Monday.

'But won't we be going round tomorrow morning with Mr Mackenzie?' Jean asked, and Pollock snapped at her, 'There are some things to sort out before he arrives. We'll meet on the women's ward at five-thirty.'

Peter Davidson, the other house surgeon on the Trauma

Unit, had just come out of the changing-room. He pulled a face after Pollock's retreating back and said gloomily, 'Ructions ahead, I fear. Tony says what's really eating old Pollock is that they could have made him acting consultant. Senior registrars do sometimes get upgraded, and it would have helped him when applying for consultant posts.'

Jean, who was kindhearted, felt very sorry for Pollock, and readily forgave him for his ill-temper. 'Then why didn't they? Why did Mr Mackenzie have to come back?'

'Who knows? Perhaps they didn't think Pollock was up to it.'

'But he's an excellent surgeon,' Jean said indignantly, and Peter nodded.

'Competent anyway. But wait till you've seen Mackenzie operating. They say even old Sir Geoffrey in his great days wasn't in his class.'

This was praise indeed, Jean knew, because Sir Geoffrey had built the Trauma Unit up until it was as famous as any in the country. They had given him a knighthood for his pioneering work, and medical knighthoods outside the big teaching hospitals were thin on the ground.

On the ward round Pollock was edgy and difficult. Jean, who had been off for the weekend, knew nothing about the fifteen or twenty emergencies who had come in on Saturday and Sunday.

'I advise you to catch up on them,' Pollock told her. 'The big chief doesn't take kindly to ill-informed juniors.'

Jean sighed, looking at the pile of case notes on the trolley. She would be lucky if she was in bed before two.

After a hasty supper she went to the office on the men's ward, and began wading through the admission notes that Peter Davidson had written up. She was still at it when her Night Sister friend, Liz Davies, looked in.

'Don't wait, Staff Nurse. I want a word with Dr Muir.' Liz slid the office door shut and sank gratefully on to a chair. 'Five minutes rest is what my poor feet need,' she said with a wink. 'What are you up to at this time of night?'

'Pollock warned me that Mr Mackenzie expects his H.S. to be well clued up. Tell me, Liz, what's the man really like? You know him quite well, don't you?'

'I do and I don't,' Liz said ambiguously. 'I mean, I was a staff nurse on this ward when he was first appointed, so I know a good deal about his working methods.' Her nice ordinary face glowed with enthusiasm. 'He's an absolutely fabulous surgeon, but he's tough and ambitious and maybe drives his juniors too hard. If you can stand the pace you'll learn a lot from him.'

Jean didn't like the sound of Alexander Mackenzie at all. She came from a tough, ambitious family herself, and she thought she preferred kindly, gentle men like Sir Geoffrey.

When she said this to Liz the other girl laughed. 'I don't suppose Sir Geoffrey was quite so affable when he was a young man climbing the career ladder. It's easy to be nice when you've got it made.'

'But Mackenzie has it made too,' Jean pointed out. 'So why should he be such an awkward type?'

'Then it's the nature of the man, I suppose. But as I told you, he's difficult to know—hasn't got a free and easy manner like old Sir Geoff.' Liz studied her hands for a moment, her expression wry. 'As a matter of fact'—she hesitated, and then went on, colouring slightly—'when I was on the ward I had quite a thing about him.'

Jean stared, surprised. 'You mean you actually fancied him? Isn't he married?'

Liz smiled. 'No. Too busy getting to the top. Though they say he's as good as engaged now to Sefton Chalmers' daughter.' Sefton Chalmers was a big industrialist, whose factories employed half the labour force of Westhampton.

There had been a faintly wistful note in Liz's voice when she had imparted this news. Jean asked a little awkwardly, 'I hope—Liz, you're not still keen on him, are you?'

'Bless you, no.' Liz's voice was brisk. 'I'm not a complete fool. Even before Pauline Chalmers came on the scene I knew I hadn't a chance, and now'—she shrugged resignedly —'Pauline has everything. She's blonde, beautiful and rich. Honestly, isn't life unfair!' She shot back her cuff, looked horrified when she saw the time, and bounced to her feet.

'It'll be interesting to see what our Alex makes of you,' she added as she slid the door back again. 'He's never had a woman H.S. before. They do say he has a weakness for blondes. There was another girl before Pauline. Looked a bit like you, come to think of it. Smooth fair hair, tall and slim. Yes, she was very like you, so who knows!'

She ducked as Jean threw a rubber at her and slammed the door back in place. Jean smiled to herself at Liz's absurd fancies. What a place for gossip hospitals were! There had already been several attempts to link her name with various unmarried men doctors on the strength of a casual date or two.

Actually Jean at twenty-three was heart-whole and fancy free. A popular girl, she had never lacked for boy-friends, but she hadn't come within measurable distance of falling in love. She settled once more to her notes, and only when she had completed those on the men's ward did she break off for a cup of tea.

She joined the others in the office and drank up quickly, her mind on the pile of notes she still had to wade through on the women's ward. She was just about to leave when the telephone rang and Liz answered it.

'Accident? Yes, Staff? Three admissions? Right, I'll warn them on the wards. Has Mr Pollock let Theatre know? Good.' She turned to Jean. 'Work, I'm afraid. A multiple pile-up on the motorway. Staff says every couch is occupied. Mr Pollock has admitted three, but they'll have to go to Theatre first. A head injury and two lads with multiple compound fractures.'

That meant that Jean would be assisting Mr Pollock, and

afterwards she would have to expand on the brief notes that were all the harassed Accident Officer would have time to scribble. No chance to catch up on the remainder of her patients. She must try and get up to the women's ward before Mr Mackenzie's round tomorrow morning. With a bit of luck the man might start late if he had only just arrived back after two months away from the Unit. He would have correspondence to cope with, Jean thought vaguely. He would have things to discuss with his secretary probably. Yes, with a bit of luck she would have time to get sorted out, and if not, she told herself stoutly, she couldn't be in two places at once. Even Mr Mackenzie could hardly be so unreasonable as to grumble at a junior who had spent most of the night in the operating theatre.

In the end Jean didn't go to bed at all. It was six-thirty on Tuesday morning before the last patient was wheeled out of Theatre. She went up in the lift with the ward nurse and the theatre porter because she wanted to keep an eye on the blood transfusion the anaesthetist had set up.

When she was satisfied with his condition she left the ward, pausing to say hallo to old Mr Thompson, who had been in the corner bed for longer than she had been on the Unit, and was likely to be there when she left. He was a cantankerous old devil, but he showed an obvious liking for Jean, professing to be amused that anyone young and pretty should choose an arduous job like surgery.

This morning, however, he hadn't a trace of a smile for her. 'How am I, Doctor? How d'you think I am after a night without a wink of sleep? All this to-ing and fro-ing and doors banging, and them boys moaning and groaning!'

'Now, Mr Thompson,' the staff nurse said reprovingly, 'you chose to be by the door yourself. And if you've had less sleep than usual how do you think poor Doctor feels with none at all?'

'It's her job, ain't it?' Mr Thompson said unsympathetically. 'She didn't have to be a doctor, did she? I don't hold with females in medicine myself.' He was still muttering to himself as they went out, and Jean thought a little ruefully that he was right. She had no reason to grumble if she went short of sleep. Unlike some young doctors, who didn't come from medical families, she had known exactly what she was letting herself in for.

It didn't seem worth going to bed, so she ran herself a bath and lay soaking in it for a long time. Afterwards, overcome with sleepiness, she flopped on to the top of her bed in her dressing-gown and shut her eyes. Just ten minutes, she thought, and then she would go down for an early breakfast, and after that she would go up to the women's ward.

## CHAPTER TWO

The ten minutes turned into more than an hour. Worn out, Jean slept until the maid arrived, armed with vacuum cleaner and polishing materials.

'Why, miss, what's wrong?' She looked astonished to find Jean still in her bedroom at nine o'clock.

After one horrified glance at her watch Jean leapt off her bed, threw off her dressing-gown and pulled on a blouse and skirt. Haste made her ladder her tights and she fumbled around in her drawer in exasperation, looking for another pair. They were all in the same state. She had meant to buy some new ones at the weekend, but had forgotten.

She smoothed her hair down with her brush, clasped it into a ponytail and made for the door. No time for any titivating if she was to get round the ward before Mr Mackenzie arrived. No time for breakfast either, unfortunately, but she paused to grab a piece of bread and butter from the dining-room. She downed a cup of milk too, and then made her way along the main corridor towards the wards.

It was customary for the junior doctors to meet their chiefs in the entrance hall. Two or three white-coated figures stood around waiting for someone, but Jean's team weren't among them.

One of the house physicians called to her as she passed. 'You're late, Jean. The big man has already arrived!'

Dismayed, Jean raced up the stairs to the second floor. With any luck Mr Mackenzie might still be exchanging pleasantries about his trip.

Unfortunately he wasn't. He was in the small side ward where the two lads who had been admitted last night were lying. He stood at the foot of one of their beds, his back to the door, reading the operation notes.

He was a big man with shoulders too broad for the white coat he was wearing. Jean tiptoed in and stood behind Pollock and Peter Davidson, hoping that her late arrival wouldn't be noticed. There were after all quite a crowd on the ward apart from the doctors, Sister and her senior staff nurse, a physiotherapist, a social worker and several students from the neighbouring university.

Mr Mackenzie tapped the notes with a long forefinger. 'Who wrote these?'

There was a little silence and he swung round impatiently. Pollock nodded towards Jean. 'The House Surgeon. Dr Muir.'

Alexander Mackenzie frowned as he looked at her. 'Where did you spring from? You weren't on the round two minutes ago.'

He had a pronounced Scots accent, which was to be expected with a name like that. At close quarters he was decidedly formidable, a dark man with a bony intelligent face and very bright observant eyes. Jean felt herself go pink as he gave her a comprehensive look that seemed to take in her hastily done hair, and even, she could swear, the ladder in her tights.

'I'm sorry, Mr Mackenzie,' she stammered. 'I—I'm afraid I'm a little late.'

He glanced at his watch. 'Ten minutes late, Miss—er——'

'Muir,' Pollock murmured, and then, taking pity on her discomfort, 'We were up all night. She probably overslept.'

'Yes, I did,' Jean said quickly, and then blushed even deeper at the withering look Mackenzie gave her.

'The only reason for not being on a ward round is urgent work somewhere else, Miss Muir. Now about these notes'—he tapped them again—'how many pints of blood did he have?'

'Three.'

'Then why not say so?'

'An oversight because I was tired,' Jean could have said, but she didn't think that would be well received, so she mumbled an apology and made herself as inconspicuous as possible behind the men.

Peter gave her a sympathetic grin, and then they were moving on to the next bed, where fortunately there were no problems. They progressed in orderly fashion up one side of the ward and down the other.

At Mark Thompson's bed Mr Mackenzie became almost human. 'Good God, man, haven't we got rid of you yet?' he asked, smiling down at the old man. Jean, who was standing opposite him now, thought that he should smile more often, because it made him seem less alarming. He looked up at that moment and caught her staring at him, and the smile vanished.

'Bring me up to date on Mr Thompson's progress,' he said crisply.

A little nervously Jean told him why Mr Thompson was still with them. 'His fracture is slow to unite, sir. There's absolutely no callous formation yet.'

'Show me his latest X-rays.' Mackenzie held out a large hand for them and studied them thoughtfully. When he had finished he said a few cheerful words to Mr Thompson and led the way out of the ward.

Once outside he looked at them gravely. 'If that old chap ever leaves here on his own two legs I'll be surprised. He's gone downhill since I last saw him.'

He sounded genuinely regretful and Jean's heart warmed to him a little, because she had a soft spot for the cantankerous old man herself. They went into the women's ward now and she caught Peter by the sleeve of his white coat.

'I haven't had time to go round here yet. You'll have to take all the cases.'

Peter, who had been on duty last weekend, had admitted all the new patients but during the week the two house surgeons were each responsible for half the ward.

'O.K.,' he murmured. 'I'll do my best, but I wasn't expecting it, you know.'

His best turned out to be not good enough for Mr Mackenzie, who became increasingly exasperated at his junior's incompetence.

'Have you looked at this patient since you admitted her, Davidson?' he asked with an edge to his voice, and Peter shook his head unhappily.

Jean couldn't stand back and let Peter take the blame, so she spoke up. 'Actually Mrs Brown is my patient, sir.'

He threw her an irritated look. 'Then why didn't you say so instead of wasting everybody's time?'

Jean took a deep breath and thrust her hands in the pockets of her white coat. 'Because I don't know anything about her either. She was admitted at the weekend, when I was off duty . . .' Her voice tailed away at his grim expression.

'I—see. This is Tuesday, Miss Muir. Did you take yesterday off as well?'

Sarcastic beast, Jean thought. 'I was in Theatre all day,' she said stiffly. 'I simply didn't have time.'

'I'm afraid you will have to learn to make time, then, won't you?' he said coldly, and turned away from her to talk to his registrars.

The physiotherapist, a sharp thin girl who didn't get on well with Jean, gave her a malicious smile. Jean ignored her and stared intently out of the window, to be brought back to the ward round with a start, by an abrasive remark from Mr Mackenzie.

'I suggest you pay attention, Miss Muir, since you know so little about your patients.'

The physiotherapist gave a giggle, quickly suppressed when Mackenzie glared at her.

It was the most uncomfortable round Jean had ever been on, and she thought wistfully of the relaxed happy days with Sir Geoffrey. When it was over she gave a sigh of relief and followed her seniors into Sister's office for the traditional cup of coffee.

Sister, a highly competent middle-aged woman, was obviously an old friend of Mr Mackenzie's. She asked him about his visit to the States, and he answered pleasantly but briefly. Not a talkative man, unlike dear old Sir Geoffrey, and not a man to waste time either.

'That was excellent coffee, Sister, as always.' He smiled and stood up, and Jean, who was nearest to the door, slid out quickly, glad to get away.

She was halfway down the first flight of stairs when he called to her. 'Don't run off, Miss Muir. I want to talk to you.'

He came down the stairs towards her, and she gripped the banister tightly because he made her feel intensely nervous.

'I'm sorry, sir. I thought you'd finished.'

'Come to my office in'—he glanced at his watch—'half an hour. You too, Davidson.'

He went on down the stairs, followed by Pollock and Tony and Peter made an expressive gesture. 'Phew! He's worse than I expected. I don't think he was impressed by us, do you?'

'No,' Jean agreed ruefully. 'What do you suppose he wants us for?'

'A wigging, doubtless,' Peter said with a grin. 'If there hadn't been all those other people around he'd have said even more than he did.'

Peter was proved only too correct. They went together to Mackenzie's office. He was sitting at his desk reading his correspondence, and he motioned them to be seated while he finished a letter.

'Well now.' He tilted his chair back and looked from one to the other of them. 'John Pollock tells me you're not usually as bad as you were today.'

'Big of him,' Peter murmured, and froze under the older man's look.

'Please don't be flippant, Davidson. I don't expect it from my house surgeon. I'm well aware that times have changed and I wouldn't want the sort of awed respect that we used to show our chiefs. But I do demand'—his gaze fastened on Peter's sandalled feet—'a reasonable standard of dress. Have you had your hair cut since you joined the Unit?'

Peter ran his hands through his hair and gave an embarrassed smile. 'Well, actually, no, sir. I don't go for short hair myself.'

'You can grow it to your waist if you want, but only when you've left my team. Patients don't on the whole care for trendy doctors. That's all, then. You can go.'

Peter left the room with obvious relief. Jean half rose too and was told to sit down again.

'I have a lot more to say to you, Miss Muir. Davidson may be a sloppy dresser, but at least he knows his job. That wasn't exactly a scintillating performance you gave on the round, was it? Pollock tells me you joined the Trauma Unit just after I left. That makes it two months ago, long enough to get the hang of things.'

'I do usually know about my patients. It was just unfortunate that we were so busy yesterday and that I fell asleep this morning. I meant to go up to the ward and catch up on the work before your round.'

To her relief his expression relaxed a little. 'All right, Miss Muir, we'll say no more about it, but don't let it happen again. What made you pick a job like this? There aren't many women in Trauma work.'

'I have to do six months in Surgery to get registered.'

'Of course, but why pick this job?'

'I really wanted one of the general surgery jobs, but someone else got it. I thought it would be fun working for Sir Geoffrey.'

Not perhaps a tactful explanation, implying that her present post was only second best. He gave her a rather grim smile.

'Well, I can assure you, Miss Muir, it won't be—fun—working for me. You're on this unit to learn surgery, not to play about.'

Jean, who took her work very seriously, tried to retrieve her unfortunate choice of words. 'I only meant—Sir Geoffrey is such a dear old man—kindly and gentle—you know——' her voice petered out under his cold stare.

'I do know, my dear,' he said ironically. 'You thought you were going to have an easy time for six months, but owing to the old man's illness you won't after all. I am neither kindly or gentle——'

'And that's a fact,' Jean muttered under her breath, goaded by his lack of understanding.

His eyes glinted with sudden anger. 'What did you say, Miss Muir?'

'I agreed with you, sir,' Jean said quickly, her heart beginning to pound in a most alarming way. 'That you're not kind and gentle, I mean,' she added, and in an attempt to stave off his wrath, risked a tentative little smile.

He stared at her for a few moments and then to her relief he smiled back, but with a tinge of mockery. 'A woman's last resort when pushed into a corner! Feminine charm, which you have in abundance, Miss Muir, as you very well know.' His eyes travelled over her thoughtfully and she shifted uncomfortably. 'Just bear in mind, my dear, that I'm not as susceptible to a pretty face as your last chief. Off you go, I've work to do.'

Dismissed, she left with what dignity she could, having learnt a valuable lesson. If she wanted the next four months to be at all bearable she had to toe the line. Alexander Mackenzie, unlike some modern consultants, believed in keeping his juniors in their place. And he would do so not only by virtue of his seniority, but by sheer force of character.

As she walked back to her room she vowed that she would never again give him the opportunity to criticise her work. It had been an unfortunate chain of circumstances that had led to that disastrous ward round. Usually she was well up on her patients' histories, because she spent a lot of time on the wards, enjoying the human side of surgery more than her sessions in the operating theatre.

It was with considerable trepidation that she turned up in Theatre for her first list with Mr Mackenzie. They had two routine operating days, Monday and Thursday, and this Thursday's session looked like being even more gruelling than last Monday's.

Jean arrived early and was changed and chatting to one of the anaesthetists when Mr Mackenzie strode down the theatre corridor.

He raised a hand to the anaesthetist. 'Hallo, Bill. Miss Muir, bring a copy of the list into the surgeons' room, and we'll sort out who does what. I take it we have two theatres? Good.' He read through the list of operations, ticking the ones he wanted to do himself. 'Show this to Theatre Sister and tell her I'll work at the far end.' He handed Jean the list just as Pollock came in, and as she went off down the corridor she heard what he said to his senior registrar.

'John, you can have young Davidson to assist and I'll make do with little Miss Muir.'

Make do indeed! Jean fumed, considerably put out by his disparaging tone. And anyway, she would far rather have worked with Pollock, whose operating technique she was used to. At least she would only be the second assistant. The first assistant did all the important work, while the second assistant held on to retractors and provided when necessary an extra pair of hands.

She wasn't, however, allowed to remain in the background. Mr Mackenzie believed in teaching his house surgeons, and grilled her endlessly on anatomy and surgical procedure.

'Not bad, not bad at all,' he commented when she had answered a tricky question on the course of the ulnar nerve.

'Give the poor girl a break,' Tony Wilson said, casting a sympathetic look at Jean's damp forehead. 'We don't want our H.S. to have a nervous breakdown, do we?'

'No indeed,' Mackenzie agreed blandly. 'That would be most unfortunate. An old chief of mine used to take the view that house surgeons were expendable, but I like to think I'm more humane.'

Everyone laughed, even Jean, a little reluctantly. He was surprisingly relaxed for a man in the middle of a rather tricky operation, but he was, Jean realised, a superlative surgeon and a supremely confident one.

They worked from nine until one-thirty, then had a half hour off with coffee and sandwiches in the surgeons' room.

'I wish you'd take a proper lunch break in a civilised fashion,' grumbled the anaesthetist, biting disconsolately into his rather dry ham sandwich.

'Wastes too much time,' Mackenzie said. 'Once you lot get away from Theatre you're reluctant to start again.'

'Now Sir Geoffrey was an eminently civilised man. He took a good hour off.'

'Ah yes, Sir Geoffrey,' Mackenzie's eyes rested for a moment on Jean, who was sitting beside Peter on the far side of the room. 'You're not the only one who misses Sir Geoffrey, Bill. Miss Muir does too.'

He was in a remarkably good humour. Jean managed a smile, but wished he would pick on someone else to tease.

The half hour went all too quickly and then they got down to work again for another four hours. By six o'clock Jean was wilting, but her chief looked as fresh as ever. He stood impatiently, while a nurse untied the tapes of his gown.

'Hurry up, girl, I've a phone call to make.' He threw his

cap and mask into the waste bin and beckoned Jean to follow him. 'Remember to order another two pints of blood for that last patient. She lost a lot during the operation. And if her husband's in tonight tell him I can see him after the ward-round tomorrow.'

'Yes, Mr Mackenzie. And about the child who had the bone graft——'

'Not now, Miss Muir. If you have any problems ask Pollock. I've a patient to see at St Michael's,' and he shut the door of the changing-room on her.

St Michael's was the swankiest nursing-home in town, equipped with its own small but extremely efficient theatre. Jean had been taken there once by Sir Geoffrey when he had needed an assistant, and neither of his registrars were free.

She thought disapprovingly that Mr Mackenzie, like many consultants, would always put his private patients first, and said as much to Peter, when they were both relaxing in the common-room before supper.

Peter looked surprised. 'I don't think you're being quite fair. If he dashed off to St Michael's I'm sure it was a genuine emergency. Everyone says Mackenzie makes no distinction in his treatment of patients. His manner's the same to a rich woman or a charwoman.'

'You mean he's rude to them all?' Jean asked, and they both laughed.

'Honestly, though,' Peter said with sudden seriousness, 'I'm glad he's back. Life was nice and relaxing with old Sir Geoff, but we'll learn more with Mackenzie.'

Peter's assessment turned out to be fairer than hers. They were having a cup of coffee after supper when the telephone rang.

'For you, Jean,' called the house physician who had answered it.

It was Mr Mackenzie, his Scots accent very pronounced on the telephone. 'Miss Muir? Sorry I had to dash off, but there was rather a flap here. Has Pollock sorted out your problems?'

'He's off duty tonight.'

'Wilson, then? You don't know where he is? Hasn't he told switchboard where he's gone?' There was disapproval now in the deep voice.

Jean, who thought that Tony had probably nipped across the road for a pint, said hastily, 'I'm sure he's around. I just meant I haven't seen him lately.'

'Hmm! If Pollock's off I think I'll look in later. There are one or two patients about whom I'm not entirely happy. I'm just going out for a meal. Expect me around ten, Miss Muir.'

'Well, what do you know?' Jean said disgustedly. 'Doesn't he trust us to look after his blessed patients?'

'Doesn't trust Tony, probably,' said Peter. 'He's known our esteemed registrar longer than we have.'

'Tony's O.K.,' Jean said, and Peter pulled a face at her.

'Sure, he's O.K. at his job, when he's doing it, but he spends too much time chatting up the nurses. And he shouldn't really drink on duty. I think it would be a friendly act if I popped over to the pub and warned him the big man will be in later, don't you?'

Jean was doing her night round when Mr Mackenzie finally appeared. While she was charting old Mr Thompson for a sedative a hand came down on her shoulder.

'I've had a look at those two women and I think they'll do. Any problems in here?'

'No, all quiet.'

'Quiet is what it isn't,' grumbled the irrepressible Mark Thompson, and Mr Mackenzie laughed and picked up his chart.

'Dr Muir has written you up for a real knockout dose, old chap. If we gave you any more you might not wake up.'

'I often wish I wouldn't,' Mr Thompson said with a sigh.

'I'm so weary, sir.' He sounded as if he really meant it, and Jean's kind heart ached for the old man, who had no close relatives in the area to visit him.

'When you're a little more mobile, Mr Thompson,' she promised, 'I'll take you out for drives on my days off. A change of scene will make you feel better.'

The old fellow brightened. 'Will you really, miss? That'll be the day!' He nodded towards Mr Mackenzie. 'She's the best of all them young doctors, sir. And a real good-looker too. I've always fancied blondes myself.'

'Don't we all?' Mackenzie agreed, slanting an amused look at Jean's embarrassed face.

The staff nurse said briskly, 'Now that's enough, Mr Thompson! I'll thank you to be more respectful to the doctors.' She sounded scandalised, but Mackenzie left the ward grinning broadly.

Jean followed him downstairs and stopped outside the door of Night Sister's office. 'You don't want me for anything else?'

'No, Miss Muir.' He looked into the office. 'If tea's going I could do with a cup.'

Liz Davies glanced up from the desk as he came in, and jumped to her feet, looking pleased. 'Good evening, Mr Mackenzie. Nice to have you back.'

There was only one chair left and he motioned Jean into it, sitting on the edge of the desk. A couple of young doctors half rose as if to offer him their seats, but he waved them back again.

'Your need is greater than mine, boys. I hope to be in my bed before long, which is more than you lot will probably be.'

The faint sense of strain caused by the appearance of a consultant quickly disappeared. Alexander Mackenzie had a certain rugged charm when he chose to exert it. He was discussing the hospital cricket team now, in which he apparently played.

Liz, who usually turned up to support their matches, was very knowledgeable, but Jean knew nothing about the game. She picked up an evening paper and glanced through the news until Mr Mackenzie spoke to her directly.

'Not a cricket fan, Miss Muir?'

She shook her head. 'We're a rugger family. I mean, my brothers are, all four of them.'

'Any of them doctors?'

She smiled. 'Two of them. And my father.'

Tony Wilson, who had just come into the room with Peter, volunteered more detailed information. 'Jean's father is Professor Muir, sir—you know, the chap at Queen's College Hospital.'

'Is that so?' Mr Mackenzie looked at Jean, and she coloured because she felt Tony's remark had been quite uncalled-for. A modest girl, she had never been given to name-dropping, although through her family she knew many of the top men in medicine.

'Mr Mackenzie's not interested in my relations,' she murmured, but Tony said airily:

'She hates people knowing who her family are. We only found out by accident when an old Queen's student came here.'

His chief eyed the young man with disapproval. 'Then why go on about it, Wilson? I'd like a word with you, by the way.' He put his cup down and walked out, followed by a rather discomfited Tony.

The others had all left by now and Liz and Jean were on their own.

'Tony talks too much when he's had a beer,' Jean observed. 'I hope Mackenzie doesn't realise where he's been.'

'He could hardly fail to if he has any sense of smell,' Liz said with unusual tartness, because Tony had never been a favourite of hers.

'He never has more than a pint when he's on call,' Jean demurred, 'and he always tells switchboard where he is.'

Liz shrugged and changed the subject, asking Jean how she was getting on with her new chief. Jean chose her words carefully, because she had seen the way her friend lit up when Mackenzie came into the room.

'He's all right, I suppose. Takes a bit of getting used to after Sir Geoffrey. How is the old man? Have you seen him tonight?'

'Doing pretty well,' said Liz, 'but they don't want him to have any visitors except closest relatives for a few days.'

Jean would have liked to see him, but she knew that this was the usual routine for coronary patients. Next week, however, at the end of a fracture clinic, Mr Mackenzie beckoned her over to his desk.

'Sister on Intensive Care says that Sir Geoffrey is fit to visit at last. You can come with me.'

A little doubtfully she said, 'Perhaps it would be better if you went on your own.'

'Rubbish,' he said briskly. 'Nothing like a pretty face to cheer up an invalid. Why, even that old curmudgeon Mark Thompson blossoms when you smile at him.' He leant back and stretched out his long legs. 'Tea first, though. Have you laid it on, Sister?'

While he drank tea he dictated several letters to his secretary, who always sat in on the clinics. Not a man to waste any time, Jean thought, and wondered if he knew how to relax. She was beginning to get used to his methods now, and though never entirely at ease with him, had to agree with Peter that working for him was quite an experience.

She found it difficult keeping up with his long strides as they made their way down the main corridor to the Intensive Care Unit.

'What's wrong, Miss Muir? Out of training?' he asked, and she panted back at him,

'When I took on this job I didn't realise it involved long-distance running!'

The words once out she regretted them, because his reaction to that sort of cheeky remark was a little unpredictable. However, it seemed to amuse him and he slowed down obligingly.

They were ushered into Sir Geoffrey's room by Sister herself. The old man, usually so rosy-cheeked, looked a shadow of his former self, and Jean found it hard to believe that anyone could change so much in ten days. The blue eyes under bushy white brows twinkled with pleasure, though, as he looked from one to the other of them.

'Thank you for coming back so promptly, Alex my boy. I feel easier to know that you're in charge. But I'm very sorry I interrupted your course.'

'They run them every year,' Alex assured him. 'I can go back at some future date.' Mindful of Sister's instructions that the old man was not to tire himself, he did most of the talking. After five minutes they were preparing to go, and Sir Geoffrey beckoned Jean nearer to the bed.

'And how's this lad treating you, my dear? Not working you too hard, I hope?'

'No, Sir Geoffrey,' Jean murmured, intrigued by the idea that anyone could think of her formidable chief as a lad. A little smile hovered on her lips, and Mackenzie, observant as always, interpreted it correctly.

'I was one of his students, Miss Muir, so he finds it hard to believe that I'm fully adult.'

'And a real hell-raiser he was, even by medical student standards,' Sir Geoffrey chuckled reminiscently. 'Popular with the nurses too—I remember——'

'Please, Sir Geoffrey, spare my blushes!' Mackenzie held up a hand in mock alarm.

Jean looked at his dark face, so full of intelligence and vitality, and had to admit that he would be attractive to most women. Not to her, though. One could admire a man's work, and his astonishing energy, without falling a victim to his magnetic personality.

She thought rather unkindly that he was decidedly spoilt,

like many medical men. All those adoring nurses, including even well-balanced girls like Liz Davies!

He put a hand on her arm and piloted her towards the door. Outside he commented, 'Sir Geoffrey's inclined to be garrulous. A sign of advancing age, I fear.'

Her affection for the old man made her speak sharply at the implied criticism.

'He's one of the kindest men I know, and—and it was a very great honour to work for him.'

He looked irritated for a moment, then shrugged his broad shoulders. 'Why can women never be objective? It is a fact—the old man is garrulous. I'm quite as fond of him as you are, Miss Muir, so don't look at me with that prim and disapproving expression. You turn it on all too frequently when I'm around.'

## CHAPTER THREE

JEAN had decided not to go home on her next free weekend. The residents were giving a farewell party to three of their number who were moving on to other hospitals, and she wanted to be there. She got up delightfully late on the Saturday morning, and went downstairs to the dining-room. Breakfast was long over, but coffee would be available at this hour.

There were several housemen at the long table, heatedly discussing one of their interminable medical problems, and at the far end a blonde girl, sitting on her own. Someone's wife or girl-friend, probably. Jean poured coffee and sat down opposite her with a smile.

'I don't think we've met before? I'm Dr Muir.'

The girl stopped in the act of raising her coffee cup to her lips. She stared at Jean, but didn't give her an answering smile.

'So you're Alex's new house surgeon! He told me he had a woman this time.'

Her tone implied that Mr Mackenzie didn't care for women colleagues, and Jean was a little put out by it. 'You're a relative of his?' she asked for something to say, and the girl laughed.

'Just a friend, Dr Muir. My name's Pauline Chalmers.'

Of course! The girl Liz had told her about, who had a rich industrialist father. Liz had also said she was beautiful, but Jean didn't quite agree. Beautifully dressed, certainly, with expertly cut hair and flawless make-up, but the sum total didn't add up, in Jean's opinion, to beauty. Her expression wasn't entirely pleasant. The blue eyes assessing her were lacking in warmth.

Pauline sipped her coffee and glanced at her watch.

'What can Alex be doing? He arranged to meet me at eleven.'

'He usually does a quick ward round on Saturday mornings, Miss Chalmers. There are so many problems that can crop up unexpectedly.'

'Don't I know it.' Pauline's smooth face was momentarily irritated. 'It beats me why you people want to be doctors.'

'What do you do?'

The girl gave her a rather superior smile. 'Do? I don't have to do anything, Dr Muir.'

'No, I suppose you don't, but I should hate to sit at home and do nothing,' Jean said coolly, nettled by her manner.

Pauline's eyes narrowed, and she seemed about to make a sharp retort, when Alexander Mackenzie walked in, accompanied by Tony Wilson and Peter.

At once Pauline jumped to her feet. 'Alex darling, I've been waiting ages. Shall we go?'

'I could do with a cup of coffee first,' he said, and sat down beside them, giving a nod in Jean's direction. 'You two have introduced yourselves, I take it?'

Jean contented herself with a brief 'Yes', but Pauline said disagreeably, 'We have indeed. Dr Muir was just upbraiding me for being a social parasite!'

Mackenzie looked astonished. 'My dear Pauline!' He glanced at Jean, for once at a loss for words.

Jean, colouring, said, 'Oh, really, Miss Chalmers, I didn't say that. I only meant——'

'I know exactly what you meant,' Pauline said, her voice honey-sweet again, and at that moment Peter put a cup of coffee down in front of his chief, and the awkward moment passed.

Mackenzie had a few last-minute instructions for his juniors and while he talked Jean drank her coffee quickly, anxious to get away. She was still feeling rather embarrassed. There was no doubt that she had offended Pauline, who was now deliberately ignoring her. It was unfortunate, but the chance that they would meet again wasn't very great. She had never seen Pauline in the doctors' mess before.

Jean rose and made her departure. No need to say anything, because they were engrossed in conversation and didn't look up. She was meeting Liz for a shopping expedition and then they were going on to Liz's home for the rest of the day.

She arrived first and was sitting in her car waiting, when Mackenzie and Miss Chalmers appeared. The girl had her hand on his arm and her face was alight with that unmistakable look of someone in love. Mackenzie's expression was amused and faintly indulgent. Impossible to tell whether he reciprocated her feelings.

Liz arrived, dashing past them and giving them a breathless, 'Good morning.'

'Am I late? Sorry, Jean. I decided to wash my hair.'

It was always a little untidy and now it looked positively frizzy. Liz smoothed it down with total lack of selfconsciousness, and Mr Mackenzie, unlocking his car, gave her a smiling glance.

'Off duty, Sister Davies? You've earned it after the last few nights.'

They had been exceptionally busy ones and Liz had certainly earned her respite. Pauline smiled too, with a friendliness she hadn't showed towards Jean.

'You poor girl. Night duty must be absolutely frightful!'

Liz murmured something and got in beside Jean. A blue estate car was parked too close to them, so Jean backed out carefully, swinging sharply to her left to avoid it.

'Mind,' Liz warned, 'you're mighty close to the big chief!'

Jean looked out through Liz's window and saw that she was only a foot away from Mackenzie's car. He was holding the door for Pauline and glanced round at her.

'Careful, Miss Muir. You won't get a good reference if you dent my new Jag!'

Flustered, Jean clashed her gears before getting into first, and he winced exaggeratedly. 'Women drivers!' he observed to no one in particular, and as she drove off Jean caught the superior smile on Pauline's face.

'Bitch!' she muttered, and Liz looked surprised.

'Who? Oh, you mean Pauline Chalmers. Have you met her, then?'

'Just briefly, and I don't think she took to me. She was quite gracious to you, though.'

Liz nodded wisely. 'Of course. I'm plain, you're pretty. She's that sort of girl.'

Jean pondered this remark. 'But, Liz, really—that's absurd. She can't be very sure of him, can she?'

'She has everything on her side,' Liz said enviously, and Jean gave her friend an affectionate glance.

'I wish you wouldn't keep on about being plain, Liz. You have character and personality and you're worth ten of girls like Pauline.'

'Unfortunately,' Liz said with dry self-mockery, 'men don't seem to be aware of it,' and then they changed the subject and started to discuss the clothes they were planning to buy.

The residents' party had started in the sitting-room, but as always it had overflowed into the dining-room and the hall and the kitchen. Jean, arriving late with Liz, felt deafened by the noise of music and laughter, and half blinded by tobacco smoke.

Pollock detached himself from the wall he was leaning against, his face rather glum.

'Wouldn't you think medical types would know better? Half of them smoking like chimneys,' he grunted. He got drinks for them and stood chatting, and presently Liz went off to dance.

'Isn't your wife here?' Jean asked.

'We couldn't find a child-minder. She's not madly keen on medical parties anyway.'

The look he directed towards his rowdier colleagues implied that he wasn't either. Jean, who liked him, was sure that his increasing moroseness was due to his worries over promotion.

'Have you any interviews coming up?' she asked, and he sighed and nodded.

'One next week, but I don't suppose I'll be lucky. The competition's so fierce unless you have the right sort of backing.'

'But you have lots of experience,' Jean said earnestly. 'And Sir Geoffrey's name counts, surely?'

'Oh, sure,' Pollock said bitterly, 'but I have to have three good reports.'

Jean was shocked. 'You mean he hasn't given you a good reference? But that's very mean.'

'Oh, I haven't seen his reference, naturally, that goes direct to the Regional Board, but he as good as told me it was a waste of time applying for a consultant post. So if he has that sort of opinion of me his reference won't be very enthusiastic, will it?'

'What a beastly man he is!' Jean burst out, and Pollock gave a quick glance round.

'Hush! Let's not say anything more——' He gave her a rather strained smile. 'But I do appreciate your sympathy, Jean dear.'

'What are you two in a huddle about?' That was Tony, elbowing his way with scant ceremony through the crowd. 'Come and dance, Jean.' He flicked an approving look over her. 'You look fabulous. That gear never came from Westhampton.'

It was an amber-coloured silk dress from a London boutique, and Jean knew that it suited her. 'Thanks, Tony,' she smiled, and slipped into his arms.

They danced well together, though hampered by lack of space. Tony, who had swapped his off-duty, had had a good deal to drink. He held Jean close and murmured outrageous compliments in her ear. Jean, who knew him of old, laughed and took them in her stride. 'Oh, honestly, Tony! Don't go on so. I'm not one of your girfriends in London.'

'Gossip,' Tony said severely, 'is the hallmark of a small mind. Who's been discussing me with you?'

'Everyone knows about your girls, Tony.' Jean smiled up at him, but he didn't return her smile.

'You're prettier than any of them. Fresher, somehow. You have a sort of budding look. Maybe because you're a budding doctor.'

He laughed at his own rather feeble joke and his grip tightened. Jean gave a little gasp. 'Tony, you've had too much to drink.'

'Maybe. Let's go and sober up with some coffee, then.'

He guided her in the direction of the door, and his arm was still round her as they went out. On the stairs coming up were Alexander Mackenzie and one of the anaesthetists. Jean, very conscious of Tony's encircling arm and wishing he would remove it, murmured, 'Good evening.'

Just for a moment Mackenzie blocked their path, his eyes going over them, then he wished them a cool good evening and went past. There was no one else in the kitchen, but a kettle was simmering gently.

'I'll make coffee,' Jean said, but Tony came up behind her and put his arms round her.

'Coffee was just an excuse,' he smiled, and turned her to face him.

He was a very attractive young man and expert at making love. Jean made a halfhearted attempt to push him away and then gave in. When he let her go she backed away, heart beating rapidly, and Tony gave a satisfied smile.

'You see, we are on the same wavelength. I always knew

it, but you're usually so aloof.'

'Because I don't trust you.' Jean busied herself making coffee with hands that trembled slightly. She had been out with lots of young men, but none of them had ever affected her as Tony had just done. His appeal was entirely physical but none the less potent for that. She felt curiously confused, half wanting him to kiss her again, half glad when another couple came into the kitchen.

Tony showed no disposition to linger now that they were not alone. Back upstairs he drifted off for a duty dance with one of his Ward Sisters, and Jean retired into a window embrasure, glad of a moment on her own.

'Hallo, Miss Muir, can I get you a drink, since your boy-friend's deserted you?'

Alexander Mackenzie stood in front of her, his expression mocking, and—there was no doubt about it—oddly hostile.

'My boy-friend? Oh, you mean Tony.' She flushed and added defensively, 'Tony's inclined to get—well—carried away at parties. It doesn't mean a thing.'

'I'm well aware of that, Miss Muir,' he said drily. 'Do you want a drink or not?'

She still felt thirsty but didn't feel like fighting her way to the bar, so she accepted his rather ungracious offer. 'I would like a long cold drink, please, non-alcoholic.'

She watched him cross the room and noticed disapprovingly how he expected and got instant attention. He was back very quickly with an orange squash for her and a beer for himself. He sat down on the broad windowsill beside her.

'I'm glad to hear that you haven't fallen for young Wilson's charm,' he remarked softly, and she gave him an indignant look.

'Honestly! I'm not a complete idiot, Mr Mackenzie.'

'I'm not suggesting you are, but clever girls have been known to make fools of themselves over men.'

'And clever men quite often pick the most unsuitable women.'

Now what on earth had made her say that? Nervousness, probably, because she wasn't given to verbal sparring.

He stared her down, his eyes cold. 'Was that remark supposed to have some significance?'

'Of—of course not,' she stammered. 'I—I was just generalising.' And she had been, but the moment she'd made it she'd thought of Pauline Chalmers, who was surely a most unsuitable match for a hard-working surgeon?

She took a large gulp of her orange squash, choked and had to suffer the indignity of being patted on the back like a child.

'Look at Pollock and Sister Winter,' he said, taking pity on her confusion. 'They make a rather incongruous pair, don't you think?'

They did indeed, as dancing partners, because Pollock was below medium height and Sister Winter was tall for a woman. They both laughed and Jean stole a quick look at him. Now was surely her chance!

'You know Mr Pollock has an interview next week?' she asked, and he nodded, his eyes still on the dancers. 'I wish he could get it,' she persisted, and he nodded again. This was discouraging, but she thought of poor Pollock, growing increasingly bitter with failure. 'He needs all the support he can get. He would feel more hopeful if you were on his side.'

She had his full attention now, and she knew that he was very annoyed although he didn't raise his voice. 'Pollock has been talking to you, Miss Muir? Complaining about me, perhaps?'

'No—not exactly.'

He gave her a sceptical look. 'I wonder. He's immersed in self-pity and ready to blame everyone but himself for his lack of success.'

'You're very ungenerous,' she retorted, stung to anger by

his insensitivity, and forgetting for a few moments the difference in their status. 'Has it ever occurred to you that he may just have been unlucky? Some good men never reach the top.'

'I have learnt something about the way of the world. And that is exactly why I tried to discourage him from applying for this particular job. He hasn't a hope of getting it, and the chip on his shoulder will grow even bigger after yet another disappointment.'

'How can you possibly tell?' she cried indignantly, and he gave an exasperated shrug.

'Because it's a plum job in a crack hospital, and one or two very bright boys are after it. When something comes up that I think he has a chance of getting, I'll back him with everything I have. Satisfied, my interfering little house surgeon?'

Reluctantly Jean conceded that there might be some truth in what he said. 'I'm ... sorry. I suppose I did talk out of turn.'

'Yes, I think you did. A famous father doesn't give you the right to treat your seniors on equal terms. And as for Pollock, he should have more pride than to discuss his affairs with you.'

But Jean hardly heard his last words, she was so mortified by his earlier remark. She had never at any time traded on her connections, and if she had been presumptuous it had been entirely due to lack of thought.

She put up her hands to her hot cheeks. 'I've said I'm sorry, Mr Mackenzie. If you'll excuse me——'

She left him abruptly and pushed her way through the crowd to Liz, who had just finished dancing with one of the medical registrars.

'Come into the other room,' Jean said, catching hold of her friend's arm. 'I don't regard it as a party when my boss is present. He's an absolutely insufferable man!'

Liz stood quite still staring over Jean's shoulder with a

look of comical dismay. Jean spun round to find Mackenzie just behind her.

He gave her a very grim smile. 'Don't worry, Miss Muir, your insufferable boss won't be stopping. But before I go how about a dance, Sister? If you're free.'

Liz gulped and nodded, and was swept away. Jean, who had by now quite lost the party spirit, went slowly upstairs to her bedroom. There was no doubt that she had made a complete fool of herself. Mr Mackenzie had never liked her, and this evening's events could have done nothing to improve his opinion of her. She wondered uneasily how he would treat her when they met again after the weekend.

# CHAPTER FOUR

SHE needn't have worried. Mr Mackenzie in Theatre was totally committed to his work and expected the same attitude from his juniors. He had no time to waste on the trivialities of personal disagreement if there was a difficult operation to be performed.

It was Pollock who was cool towards her, and Jean wondered uneasily if Mackenzie had spoken to him about their conversation at the party. Always a girl who liked to know where she stood, she tackled him at the end of the operating list.

'Is something wrong? Why are you so cross this morning?'

'There's plenty wrong. What the devil made you talk to Alex, you interfering little idiot?'

They were standing in the main corridor outside Theatre and he kept his voice down because there were other people about.

'I thought it might help. Is he very annoyed about it?'

'How the hell do I know? We haven't discussed it.'

'Then how do you know we talked about you?'

'Because, my dear girl, one of the chaps overheard you and told me all about it. Has probably told half the mess as well. What Mackenzie must think I can't imagine!'

Pollock looked both furious and unhappy, and Jean laid a placating hand on the sleeve of his white coat. 'Why not talk to him? Explain that you knew nothing about it? Or would it come better from me?'

'Oh, for God's sake,' Pollock snarled. 'You've done enough damage already!'

He jerked his arm away, but not before Mackenzie, coming through the Theatre doors with Tony and Peter, had seen them together. Pollock muttered something under his breath and went off in the other direction, and Jean followed her colleagues slowly down the corridor to the dining-room.

That evening Liz gave her a message from old Sir Geoffrey. 'He says it's ages since you visited him. He's much better and beginning to get bored. Do call in tomorrow.'

So at the end of the ward round Jean went along to the Intensive Care Unit, where Sir Geoffrey was sitting up now, propped against a nest of pillows, and listening to the radio. His cheeks had regained their usual ruddy colour, but he looked years older.

'Good of you to come, my dear. Pull that chair up. Sister's off duty, thank goodness. Watches over me like a dragon, you know.'

He puffed his cheeks out and looked pathetic. Jean laughed. 'You know quite well she does it for your own good. Are you sure it's all right, my being here?'

There was a touch of hauteur in his manner. 'If I wish to have visitors I shall. Now tell me, are you getting on better with Alex?'

'Better? How did you know we weren't getting on?'

'Asked him what he thought of you, when he was last in here. He was a bit guarded, so I guessed you weren't too friendly.'

Jean smiled at him. 'Friendly is scarcely a word that applies between a consultant and a house surgeon.'

'Nonsense! Aren't we friendly?'

'Well, yes, but that's different, because you're older. I think Mr Mackenzie's one of those men who gets on better with his own sex.'

The old man chuckled and shook his head. 'No, no, my dear! Alex isn't a misogynist. He's had lots of girl-friends. I can't think why he hasn't settled down with a wife. Have you met Pauline Chalmers, eh?'

'Once,' Jean said noncommittally, and he gave her a

shrewd look.

'Didn't take to her? Well, neither did I. Hard as nails, that one.'

'Then I should think they'd be admirably suited,' Jean said with unusual sharpness.

'My word, you really do have it in for him, don't you?'

Jean began to think that there was some truth in Mackenzie's comment on Sir Geoffrey. Age had made him garrulous and also rather indiscreet. She changed the subject and told him about an interesting case on the children's ward. She was glad she had done so when the glass door swung open and Mackenzie walked in. It would have been more than embarrassing if he had heard them discussing him.

Jean jumped up. 'I must be going.'

'No, no, don't run away,' Sir Geoffrey murmured, but Mackenzie gave one of his sarcastic smiles.

'It's not you she's running away from. Consider yourself favoured. I doubt she'd come and visit me if I was sick.'

Jean looked at him indignantly, which only made him smile the more. He dumped some books on Sir Geoffrey's bedside table.

'These are the ones I promised you.' He tapped the top of the pile. 'This one on roses is first class.'

'Are you a gardener?' Jean exclaimed, and he nodded, his expression a little wry.

'Why the surprise, Miss Muir? Does it seem out of character?'

'Unexpected anyway,' but after all, what did she know about the man? He was a dedicated surgeon, who was unsparing of himself and everybody else in the pursuit of perfection. He must have off-duty interests or he would crack under the strain.

'Interested in gardening yourself?' he asked, and she shook her head.

'Never had much opportunity. We live in the centre of

London, where nothing seems to thrive.' She looked out of the window at the busy main road that ran past the hospital, the sound of the traffic muted because they were on the fourth floor. Beyond stretched the ugly industrial landscape. 'I've always wanted to live in the country,' she added rather wistfully. 'I should hate to spend all my working life somewhere like this.'

'If you don't like this sort of place what made you come here?' Mackenzie asked.

'I do like it,' she said quickly, with the touch of defensiveness that she so often showed towards him. 'I love working at the Royal. But I shouldn't want to live in Westhampton. I suppose you have a place somewhere outside?'

'No, Miss Muir, I have a flat not far from the hospital.' At her surprised look he added, 'I do my gardening at my cottage in Shropshire. I go there most weekends.'

They were interrupted by a staff nurse with a message from Mr Pollock, who was telephoning from the Accident Department.

'They've a patient in whom he'd like you to see urgently, sir. A Mr Chalmers—Mr Sefton Chalmers.'

Mr Mackenzie rose at once, his face concerned. 'I'd better go. John doesn't send urgent messages unnecessarily.'

He went off, and Jean said goodbye to Sir Geoffrey and went down to lunch. She was finishing her coffee when Mackenzie and Pollock came in.

Mackenzie bent down to speak to Peter, who was sitting next to Jean. 'We've got an emergency lined up in Theatre, Davidson. Two o'clock sharp. It's a private patient, but we'll need a third pair of hands. You're free, I take it?'

'Yes, sir.'

The two surgeons moved on to their own table and Jean said, 'Perhaps it's Sefton Chalmers. I heard he was in the Accident Department.'

Peter whistled softly. 'Sefton Chalmers! He's stinking rich, isn't he? You'd expect him to demand one of the top

London men.'

'Perhaps he's not in a fit state to make any demands. Besides, Mackenzie's reputation is as good as any London man's.'

'Oh, sure,' Peter agreed, 'but they're said to be a very arrogant family. Mackenzie may be good enough for them, but I doubt if our private wing is.' He gave her a wink. 'Some lovely lolly, anyway. He always pays his H.S. for private cases.'

There was no compulsion on the consultants to do this. Some expected their juniors to turn up for every case and never paid a penny.

Jean said dubiously, 'But he can hardly charge a fee to friends. Perhaps it isn't Mr Chalmers anyway. Most surgeons don't like operating on people they know.'

But it was Sefton Chalmers. Jean heard the full story that evening from Peter, who had it from Pollock and the nursing staff. Mr Chalmers had been brought into the Accident Department practically exsanguinated, with multiple fractures and internal injuries. His chauffeur was dead on arrival, their car having been crushed by an articulated lorry.

So Mr Chalmers had been, as Jean had suggested, in no state to make any demands, had not indeed been identified immediately. When he was his wife and daughter were sent for urgently, and they had asked that he be put under Mr Mackenzie, although it was in fact the duty day of the other trauma surgeon.

'Mackenzie didn't want to take him on, apparently,' Peter told Jean, 'but they begged him to. They were rather sniffy, though, about the old man being in the Royal, wanted him transferred as soon as possible to St Michael's, but with that our Alex wouldn't agree. Said he would only take him on if he was in a proper hospital. St Michael's was O.K. for minor surgery, but these society nursing homes were no good for serious cases. He's right, of course. It's sheer snobbery that makes so many rich people avoid ordinary hospitals.'

'And did they agree?'

'No choice,' Peter said with a grin. 'Our Alex usually gets his own way, doesn't he?'

'And Mr Chalmers? Will he do?'

Peter shrugged. 'Fractured pelvis, fractured femur, ruptured liver and spleen! He's fifty-two, but very fit for his age, so I suppose he's got a sporting chance. He's already had ten pints of blood.'

Sefton Chalmers remained on the dangerously ill list for days. One afternoon Jean had to visit the private wing, to see a patient who had been put there because there was a shortage of beds on the general ward. As she walked down the corridor a door opened and Pauline Chalmers came out, blowing a careless kiss into the room behind her. She was beautifully turned out and perfectly made up. She stared when she saw Jean.

'I didn't realise you had anything to do with the private patients, Dr—um——?'

'Muir,' Jean supplied, and feeling something more was necessary, 'I hear your father's on the mend, Miss Chalmers. It must have been a terribly worrying time for you.'

'Oh, nothing could kill Father,' Pauline said confidently.

Perhaps she really didn't know how near he had been to death. Jean thought her incredibly cushioned against reality. Did she spend all her time on that immaculate appearance? Wasn't there any feeling beneath the surface gloss?

'How can you bear to go around in that dowdy white coat?'

The question took Jean by surprise. The regulation white coats certainly weren't smart, but on duty her mind was on her work, not on her appearance.

'I never think about it,' she admitted, and the other girl gave a rather superior smile.

'How dedicated you are, Dr Muir. It seems horribly unfeminine to me,' and she went past on an overpowering wave of perfume.

Jean scowled after her, not at all liking to be called unfeminine. She gave way to a childish urge and put her tongue out at Pauline's retreating back.

It was unfortunate that that was the precise moment that Alexander Mackenzie should emerge from one of the other rooms, bang in front of her.

He gave her an astonished look, and then caught sight of Pauline just before she turned the corner. Beneath his sardonic gaze her colour mounted furiously. 'H-hallo, Mr Mackenzie. I—I'm just going to see Mrs Williams. You know—the ward p-patient that they put in here.'

'You're babbling, Miss Muir,' he commented unkindly. 'And you have every reason to be embarrassed, behaving in such a childish fashion. What has poor Pauline done now?'

He was presumably referring to that other incident in the doctors' dining-room.

'Poor Pauline indeed!' Jean snapped, too ruffled to be discreet, and then as his lips tightened, 'I'm sorry, I know she's a friend of yours, but why does she always have to be so darned patronising?'

His eyebrows went up. 'Patronising? In what way?'

'She called me unfeminine,' Jean said crossly, and then at his look of growing amusement, 'Well, after all, I may be a doctor, but that doesn't mean that I'm unfeminine, surely?'

His eyes travelled slowly from the top of her smooth blonde head down to her slim and shapely legs, and something about the way he looked at her made her go an even deeper red.

'Cheer up, little one, you are most definitely not unfeminine. In fact when you grow up you'll be quite a woman!'

Jean hated being laughed at. She gave him a furious

glare, which only increased his amusement.

'Has anyone told you how beautiful you look when you're angry?' and then with a sudden change of tone, 'This is all highly unprofessional, anyway. We'll go and see that patient together.'

He was once more the consultant and he strode down the corridor, followed by Jean, who was aware that it was entirely her own fault if she had been made to look foolish. What really rankled was the implication that Mr Mackenzie considered her immature.

She told Peter about it at supper and he was hugely amused.

'Not to worry,' he said consolingly. 'He was just putting you in your place because you were rude to his bird. And she tries to patronise you because she regards you as a threat.'

Jean didn't pretend to misunderstand him. 'Oh, Peter, really! I don't even like the man. You're getting to be a worse gossip than some of the nurses!'

'I thrive on gossip,' Peter said cheerfully, and at that moment Tony joined them.

'What gossip? What have I missed?'

'You two!' Jean exclaimed, laughing. 'It's a pure myth that women are the ones who gossip. Men are every bit as bad when they live in places like hospitals.'

'Well, let's give them something to gossip about,' Tony suggested. 'You're off this evening and so am I. I'll take you for a drive. O.K.?'

Jean looked at him a little doubtfully. She hadn't been alone with him since the night of the party, but she remembered vividly the effect he had had on her. A drive with Tony would certainly include a session of lovemaking. Was it possible to be strongly attracted to a man of whom you didn't at all approve? Didn't she run the risk of being hurt if she got too involved?

Tony had been studying her while she sat in silence. 'It's

only a drive I'm suggesting, darling. Does it require quite such weighty consideration?'

His eyes mocked her and she knew that he was well aware of what she had been thinking. It was a lovely evening and a few hours away from the hospital would be a welcome change.

'All right,' Jean said, and Tony laughed, not at all put out by her lack of enthusiasm. He had numerous faults, but vanity wasn't one of them.

'I get the message quite plainly,' he told her as they walked to his car. 'Necking is out—at least for tonight.'

'Oh, Tony, you are an idiot,' Jean smiled, relaxing at once. Something made her add, 'Have you ever been in love? Really in love?'

His usually good-humoured face twisted into bitter lines. 'Once,' he said quietly, 'but she gave me the push. Said I was unreliable. The trouble about women is that they get so possessive.'

At least he was honest, Jean thought, and she had had fair warning. It would be madness to let herself get too fond of a casual character like Tony.

He kept his word. They drove for miles to one of his favourite haunts, a delightful pub on the banks of the River Severn, where you could sit on a stone-flagged terrace and watch the boats go by. They were both a little tired after a hard day's work, and content to watch other people being more energetic.

Jean leant her head against the back of her chair and smiled at Tony through half-shut eyes. 'It's very pleasant here,' she murmured, and Tony nodded.

'Yes, it is. And stop looking at me like that or I shall forget all my good resolutions. For such a pretty girl you seem singularly unaware of the effect you have on men.'

He put his hand on her bare arm and stroked it softly. She sat up quickly, and as she did so a boat drew into the little jetty belonging to the inn. Alexander Mackenzie stepped out of it, extending a helping hand to his companion.

'Well, look who's here!' Tony exclaimed. 'Our esteemed chief and his favourite bird! I suppose she's quite something if you like the type.'

Pauline was wearing a beautifully cut linen suit that must have cost the earth. Jean couldn't resist asking, 'And what type is that?'

'Cold. Hard. Selfish,' said Tony. 'You wouldn't think an intelligent man like Mackenzie could be fooled by her, would you?'

'Perhaps he isn't. But she is very striking, after all. Maybe it flatters his vanity to be seen with her.'

Tony shrugged. 'Maybe. Though I shouldn't have thought his ego needed that sort of boost.'

Mackenzie had paid off the boatman and now they were strolling up from the jetty. Jean said under her breath, 'I hope they go inside,' but they came up the steps and Mackenzie stopped by their table.

'Hallo, you two. May we join you?'

'Of course.' Tony jumped up to pull out a chair for Pauline, who looked no more pleased than Jean felt at this unexpected meeting.

Mackenzie went off for their drinks and Jean watched in amazement while Tony, who had just delivered such an unkind assessment of Pauline's character, put himself out to be charming to the girl. Her rather sulky expression cleared and she responded animatedly to Tony's lighthearted flirtation.

The two of them monopolised most of the conversation. Jean was quite content to take a back seat, but she was a little put out when Mackenzie leant towards her.

'Why so quiet, Miss Muir?' he asked under his breath. 'Could it be that you're a wee bit jealous?'

She stared at him, taking a few seconds to grasp his meaning. Then she said coolly, 'I'm not with you, Mr Mackenzie.'

'Oh yes, you are,' he countered swiftly. 'Your boy-friend is neglecting you, and well you know it.'

'I've already told you'—her voice had risen so she broke off and continued more softly—'he is not my boy-friend.'

'He was giving a very good imitation of one when we arrived.'

Tony interrupted them to suggest another round of drinks. 'I'll come with you,' Pauline offered, and as the two of them disappeared inside Jean couldn't resist a counter-attack.

'Perhaps you're a wee bit jealous too?' She gave him her demurest smile, but she might have known she couldn't win.

'No, Miss Muir,' he replied pleasantly. 'I don't take women seriously enough for that.'

She gave a little gasp. 'Honestly—what arrogance! Men!'

'Not Pauline's type of woman anyhow,' he amended with surprising frankness, and Jean felt, rather unexpectedly, a touch of pity for the girl.

'Poor Pauline,' she said quietly, and saw the surprise in his eyes.

'I thought you didn't like her.'

'I don't particularly,' Jean said honestly. 'But if she's fond of you she'll get hurt. Men are so cynical.'

'It's women that make them so. And this conversation is beginning to get out of hand, a thing that seems to happen when you've had a drink or two.'

She blushed and said quickly, 'You're thinking of the party?' She was trying to make up her mind whether to say something about Pollock, when the other two returned and conversation became general once more.

At least the other three talked and Jean said very little, until Mr Mackenzie giving her a searching look, said, 'Our little house surgeon can hardly keep her eyes open, Wilson. Don't you think it's time you took her back to the hospital?'

Disgustedly Pauline said, 'But it's not yet ten. Let's stay a little longer, darling.'

'We can, if you want,' Mackenzie agreed. 'It's Jean whom I think should go to bed. She has a busy day ahead of her tomorrow.'

'Doing what?' Pauline asked, while Jean registered the fact that it was the first time he had used her christian name.

'Standing for nine or ten hours in an operating theatre. Tiring enough for a man, more so, I imagine, for a young girl.'

'Then why does she do it?' Pauline's blue eyes held Jean's for a moment and there was no doubt about the hostility in them.

'Why indeed?' Mackenzie said casually. 'Care to enlighten us, little one?'

There was no real interest in his question. It just amused him to bait her. It was probably for the same reason that he had joined them in the first place.

'No, I don't care to,' she said, and got quickly to her feet. 'You're right, I am tired. Do you mind, Tony?'

Tony, who seemed disposed to linger, responded very decently to her appealing look. As they turned away he slipped a hand through her arm in a rather proprietorial way, and Jean caught once again the curiously disapproving look on her chief's face.

'So Pauline's not as bad as you thought, Tony?' she asked teasingly as they walked to the car.

Tony took his time about replying. 'She's probably just as bad as I thought, but she's very attractive, as even you must agree. And she understands the rules of the game, which is more than you do, my sweet.'

Jean was getting tired of being treated as a child. 'Oh, I understand them all right,' she told him sharply. 'I just don't want to play.'

'Am I to take it from that,' Tony asked with mock ruefulness, 'that stopping in a quiet spot is out? It is? Oh well...'

He took it with his usual lightheartedness, whistling softly to himself as he eased the car out of the parking lot on to the main road.

Jean, who really was tired, rested her head back and shut her eyes. Annoyingly her thoughts were of Mr Mackenzie and why he appeared to disapprove of her friendship with Tony. Or was it simply that he disliked her so much that whatever she did was wrong?

On this rather disquieting idea she nodded off and didn't wake up until they reached the hospital. The car park was deserted and quite dark. She sat up sleepily just as Tony pulled her into his arms and put his mouth on hers.

'A reward for good behaviour,' he said with a smile, and let her go again. 'Sleep well, and don't brood on your missed opportunities!'

## CHAPTER FIVE

JEAN usually started her night round at ten o'clock. One evening, when she had seen about half the patients on the women's ward, she was called to the telephone urgently.

A flustered voice the other end announced itself as Staff Nurse Humphrey from Private Wing.

'We need you urgently, Doctor. It's Mr Chalmers, Room Four.'

'I don't look after private patients, Staff. You'd better ring Mr Mackenzie.'

'We've done that, and he's out.' The girl's voice sounded distraught. 'It's really urgent, Doctor. He's had an accident, bleeding badly. Please come!'

Whether it was your patient or not, you answered a call like that. 'I'll be down at once,' Jean said reassuringly. 'Have you rung Night Sister?'

'Sister Davies is already here. She told me to ring you.'

'I'll be down,' Jean said again, and rang off. 'Trouble,' she told the nurse on Female Orthopaedic. 'But I'll be back as soon as possible.'

She was puzzled as to what sort of accident a man still confined to his bed could have had, and she wondered why Liz hadn't contacted the registrar on duty, but questions could wait until later.

She took the stairs two at a time, because the lift was on another floor, and arrived in the private wing just as a young nurse was pushing a trolley through the door of Room Four. It hadn't the usual neat appearance of a private room. There was an overturned vase on the floor and a broken glass, and a lot of blood on the bedside rug. There was blood on the sheets too, and Mr Chalmers lay back against the pillows, ashen-faced. On the bedside table stood a whisky bottle, rather surprisingly.

Liz, calm as ever in the centre of chaos, was pressing hard on his wrist, but a steady trickle of blood escaped from an ugly laceration in the man's right palm.

'I think he's cut a small artery,' she told Jean. 'Lost quite a bit before we arrived. Mr Mackenzie's not obtainable and we can't find Dr Wilson. We'll go on trying, but we can't leave him like this, can we?'

Mr Chalmers was frightened and in pain, and it didn't make it any easier to deal with him. Jean hadn't met him before. As she bent over to have a closer look at the wound she said quietly, 'I'm Mr Mackenzie's house surgeon, Mr Chalmers. He'll be along as soon as they can find him, but I'm going to try and stop the bleeding.'

She probed the wound gently and then put a thick wad of gauze and wool over it, and bound the lot up very tightly. To Liz she said, 'Elevate his arm and give him a sedative—fortral, I think. Could be worse. I don't think he's cut any tendons and there doesn't seem to be any glass in it. We'll hope Mr Mackenzie comes soon and he can sew it up himself.'

She spoke softly, but Mr Chalmers heard her. 'Not up to it?' he growled. 'Too difficult, eh?'

She turned to look at him. A little colour was coming back into his face, and she thought what a bad-tempered face it was. Pauline had certainly not inherited her looks from him. His features were heavy, his complexion rather coarse. He didn't look a nice man, but he was a patient and had to be humoured.

'I should be quite happy to do it, Mr Chalmers,' she said evenly, 'and I should if you were on the ward, but private patients are generally left to our chiefs. I've written you up for a sedative, and I'll come and see you again in a quarter of an hour if they haven't located Mr Mackenzie. Sooner if he begins to bleed badly again,' she added softly to Liz.

But Mr Mackenzie couldn't be found. Jean wondered

whether to consult the senior orthopaedic surgeon, but decided against it.

'I think I'd better put some stitches in myself,' she told Mr Chalmers. 'You'll feel the local anaesthetic, but after that it won't hurt.'

'About time someone did something,' he grumbled.

Jean ignored him and concentrated on scrubbing her hands thoroughly. When she had injected the local anaesthetic she had to wait five minutes for it to take effect. The room had been tidied since she was last in it, the rug and the blood-stained bedclothes replaced. She remembered the glass on the floor and the strong smell of whisky.

'What happened?' she asked, and Liz with a rather grim face referred her to Mr Chalmers.

'I was trying to pour myself a Scotch,' he said glumly, 'and I knocked the glass over. I didn't realise it was broken till I jabbed my palm on the sharp edge.'

'Mr Chalmers hasn't mentioned that he had a bottle of whisky hidden away in his locker,' Liz said in her most forbidding voice. 'Quite against regulations, of course.'

'Now see here, young woman——'

'I don't think you should agitate yourself,' Jean cut in swiftly. 'You might feel faint again,' she added, wondering if he glared as fiercely at his staff.

'Tony should be on call. Where is he?' she muttered under her breath, and Liz shrugged.

'That young man can never be found when he's really wanted. Your five minutes are up now.'

So Jean started probing the wound more carefully, having first ascertained that he could feel no pain. She tied the spurting artery with a ligature and put in a neat row of black silk stitches, to a running commentary of grumbles from Mr Chalmers.

When Liz had cut the last stitch Jean tossed her instruments into the metal bowl on the trolley, and went over to the sink to wash her hands.

'He's all yours, Sister,' she snapped, 'and I wish you well of him!'

Liz's eyes opened very wide, because however provoking Mr Chalmers had been he was after all a private patient and a very important local man.

'What's that? What's that? Are you trying to be offensive, young woman?'

'Yes, I am,' Jean said in exasperation. 'But I don't suppose I could equal you at it. You're a very rude, disagreeable, ungrateful old man. You give yourself a nasty injury entirely through your own fault, and then when we try to help you, you treat us like dirt!'

She had never seen anyone go so red, alarmingly red, but mercifully he was too astonished to answer her. He stuttered incoherently and she took advantage of it to get in a parting shot as she turned towards the door.

'Sleep well, Mr Chalmers. I don't think Mr Mackenzie will be a bit pleased when he hears about the whisky.'

The door opened on her last words and Alexander Mackenzie came in. 'What the devil is going on?' he asked.

'Mr Chalmers had an accident.' That was Liz stepping in quickly.

'No one has ever spoken to me like that in my life!' That was Sefton Chalmers, who had finally recovered his voice. He pointed a trembling finger at Jean. 'Alex, that girl of yours is the rudest young woman I've ever met. She deserves to be sacked for her impertinence!'

Mackenzie picked up the industrialist's hand and examined the wound. 'She's sewn you up very neatly, though, old chap,' he said pleasantly. 'Suppose you tell me what it's all about. And you had better make yourself scarce Miss Muir,' he said softly, without turning round. 'Dressing, please, Sister.'

Jean went out quickly, her temper already cooled sufficiently for her to regret losing it. Junior residents, however much they were provoked, weren't expected to be rude to private patients. On the rare occasions when they came in contact with them, they stood a pace or two behind their chiefs and maintained a discreet silence.

'But after all, tonight was different,' Jean said, when recounting this extraordinary episode to Peter and Tony a few minutes later in the Night Sisters' office. 'I had to do something or he would have lost a lot of blood. Surely Mackenzie should be grateful?'

She was trying to reassure herself, and Peter, a nice lad, did his best to abet her.

'Of course he should be. I doubt if I'd have had the nerve to sew up a private patient.'

'That was just why I didn't want to do it. He probably wouldn't have made such a fuss if someone more senior had done it. Where were you, anyway, Tony?'

'In the library, reading the surgical journals,' Tony said virtuously.

'You ought to tell switchboard where you are,' Jean said a little crossly. 'I must get back to the ward. With a bit of luck I shan't see Mackenzie till Monday, by which time things will have blown over.'

She was out of luck, however. Mackenzie and Liz were talking in the corridor just outside the office. Jean went past them, hoping he might be too preoccupied to notice her, but he put out a long arm and caught her by the wrist.

'Don't rush off, Miss Muir. I have something to say to you.'

'I haven't finished my night round yet,' Jean said hopefully. 'Staff is waiting for me to write up some drugs.'

'Then she can wait a few minutes longer. Come in here for a moment. You too, please, Sister.'

'Here' was a small room where relatives sometimes waited, now empty. He shut the door behind them and leant against it.

Jean looked at Liz, who kept her eyes down, a worried expression on her usually tranquil face.

'Well, Miss Muir? I feel you've some explaining to do.'

It was difficult to tell from his manner just how annoyed he was. He had the rather unnerving characteristic of remaining impassive until he had heard all sides of the question. Only then, if it was justified, did he explode into wrath.

Jean, who wasn't by nature timid, found him an alarming man. It was a quality that belonged to him as a person, and had nothing to do with his position in the hospital hierarchy.

'H-hasn't Sister Davies explained what happened?' she stammered.

'She has, and so has Mr Chalmers, exhaustively, but I want your version. Come on, girl, or we'll be here all night.'

He sounded irritated rather than angry, so Jean plucked up courage and told him her side of the story.

'I know I spoke out of turn, but he was being very unco-operative and—and overbearing. I was a bit rattled anyway because I wasn't sure if I was doing the right thing. Interfering with a private patient at all, and—and not doing it in Theatre.'

She spread out her hands in an unconscious gesture of appeal, and gave him a propitiatory smile. He didn't smile back, but there was a hint of amusement in his voice when he answered.

'Of course you did the right thing, and of course it was better to do him in his room. He isn't fit for unnecessary moving around. But calling him a rude, disagreeable, ungrateful old man! I shouldn't think anyone has ever spoken to him like that in his entire life. As a matter of fact I think it's the *old* that rankles most!' he ended on a laugh.

Jean took courage from his manner. 'Sister told you about the whisky?'

'She did, and I've torn strips off him, but it's my job to do that, not yours. So don't make a habit of being rude to my patients.' He opened the door and stood aside for them. 'You'd better get back to your ward now. And first thing tomorrow morning you can go up to see Mr Chalmers.'

'See him?' Jean stared at him blankly.

'See him. At his request.'

'But——'

'No buts, my girl. First thing tomorrow. That's an order.'

So next morning after breakfast Jean went, very reluctantly, up to the private wing and called in at Sister's office.

'Mr Mackenzie asked me to look in on Mr Chalmers. Would this be a convenient time?'

Sister, a smart brunette with an assured manner, didn't bother to conceal her amusement. 'I heard about your little disagreement, Doctor. He's a thorough nuisance, in my opinion, but money talks, doesn't it? It would never occur to him that he was in the wrong.'

She seemed to take it for granted that Jean had come to apologise, and disappeared tactfully, once she had seen that Mr Chalmers was presentable.

He looked better this morning, freshly shaved and his bed newly tidied, a neat pile of official-looking documents on his bed table. He had one in his hand when Jean came in and lowered it to look at her.

Last night she had thought him just a bully, blustering as bullies do, because he knew himself to be in the wrong. Today she could understand why his was a name to mention with respect. The light eyes beneath bushy grey eyebrows were shrewd and compelling. When he spoke it was quietly and with authority.

'Well, young lady, it seems we both lost our tempers last night. I owe you an apology. Alex says you did a fine job on my hand.'

This unexpectedly handsome tribute took Jean completely by surprise. She was silent so long that Sefton Chalmers began to frown rather forbiddingly.

'Well?' he growled. 'Not satisfied? You should be. I can't remember when I last apologised to anyone.' He lay back against his pillows, those disconcerting eyes assessing her very thoroughly.

Relief at the way the interview was going made Jean relax. 'Of course I'm satisfied. I think it's very decent of you, and—and rather unexpected too.'

'Why unexpected?' he shot back at her.

She gave him her most disarming smile, convinced now that he wasn't nearly as disagreeable as he was reputed to be. 'Because after all, I was rude too. I should have made more allowance for the shock you'd had.' She looked at his bandaged hand. 'I hope it's not too painful?'

'Hardly hurts at all,' he assured her. 'But Alex tells me I mustn't use it for several days, which is a damned nuisance. I've a lot of paperwork to catch up on.'

Which a man who had been so ill shouldn't really be doing. However, he probably had the sort of temperament that was not suited to idleness.

'I won't waste your time, then,' Jean said, and suddenly, impulsively she put out her hand, and he put his good one in hers. 'Goodbye, Mr Chalmers. I hope you're soon on your feet again.'

'Not a hope,' he said gloomily. 'Alex says I'll be on my back for quite a bit longer. So you can come and see me again, eh?'

'I will, Mr Chalmers.'

'Good, Dr Muir. And what's a pretty young thing like you doing in this sort of work anyway?'

It was a question Jean had often been asked and she turned it off lightly and made her departure, to ponder on the surprising fact that Sefton Chalmers, far from being a disagreeable bully, was rather a dear.

'So you've made another conquest, Miss Muir? It beats me how you do it.'

Alexander Mackenzie gave his house surgeon an ironic smile as they sat in the surgeons' room having coffee next operating day.

'I'm sorry, I don't quite understand,' Jean murmured.

'Our leading industrialist, little one,' he said softly. He was sitting next to her, his long legs stretched out in front of him.

Tony, stepping over them carefully, caught the drift of the conversation. 'Nothing odd about it, sir,' he chipped in. 'Most men go for dishy blondes. You'd better watch out, Jean! Sefton Chalmers has a reputation for being a fast worker with women!'

'Oh, for God's sake, Wilson! The man's old enough to be her father! And who the devil asked for your opinion?'

Tony, suitably squashed, retired hastily, watched with a frown by Mackenzie. It occurred to Jean, not for the first time, that their chief didn't care for his junior registrar.

'Sefton's quite lost his heart to you, Miss Muir. I gather it was a most touching scene, with both of you anxious to make it up?'

He was teasing her, of course, but there was something a little disagreeable about his manner.

'You told me to go and see him,' Jean answered, 'and he wasn't at all like I expected. He was absolutely sweet.'

He gave a snort of contemptuous laughter. 'Sweet! Dear heaven, what a word to apply to Sefton! Singularly inappropriate, in my opinion.'

'He was sweet to me,' Jean said with a touch of obstinacy. 'I think his reputation is probably grossly exaggerated.'

'No, my dear, it isn't. He is every bit as arrogant and ruthless as he's made out to be.'

'I thought you were a friend of his.'

'No, I'm a friend of his daughter's. I wouldn't have taken him on if I'd known him well.'

He rose, and his juniors rose reluctantly, because he never gave them a long enough coffee break.

'Tell them to ring for the next patient, Davidson. We've a busy day ahead of us. I think we'll have to cut out coffee in future.'

# CHAPTER SIX

JUNE had come in wet and rather cool, but on Jean's next half day the weather was perfect. After lunch she changed into a shirt and trousers with the vague idea of going out for a drive.

Nobody seemed to be free and she didn't fancy a solo outing. She stretched out a little disconsolately on the sofa in the empty sitting-room, while she tried to decide what to do. This was one of the times when a job nearer home, within reach of family and friends, would have been an advantage.

She had been up half the night and felt rather sleepy, so she shut her eyes and in no time had drifted off. She woke again with a start, to find Mr Mackenzie standing over her, his hands on the sofa back, regarding her quizzically.

She sat up quickly, pushing her hair out of her eyes. 'I'm off duty,' she said with a touch of defensiveness, in case he should make some sarcastic remark about idle house surgeons.

'Relax, Miss Muir, I know it's your half day. Sorry I woke you. I'm looking for Pollock.'

'He went home for lunch.'

'It can wait. What the devil are you doing indoors on a lovely day like this? You should be out in the sunshine.'

'I was trying to decide where to go and I dozed off.'

He gave her a sardonic smile. 'Boy-friend not available today? Taking his wife out for a change?'

She stared at him in complete bewilderment, and he made a quick annoyed gesture as he turned towards the door. 'Oh, forget it. It's not my affair anyway.'

'Forget what? What are you talking about?'

'You know perfectly well what I'm talking about,' he

said with extreme coldness. 'Even in this permissive age decent girls don't run after married men.'

Pollock? Jean thought confusedly. Could he possibly think she was interested in Pollock? The idea was ludicrous.

'You've got it all wrong,' she assured him, trying hard not to laugh. 'I only take an interest in Pollock's affairs because I'm sorry for him.'

'I am not talking about Pollock. I'm talking about Tony Wilson, as you very well know.'

'Tony!' she exclaimed. 'But he's not married! Whatever gave you that idea?'

He was frowning now, and watching her steadily. 'We happen to have a mutual acquaintance, Wilson and I. A chap who worked at his last hospital and felt sorry for his wife. Asked me once if Wilson still fooled around with other women. Oh, he's married all right——' His eyes narrowed as he looked at her shocked face. 'So it wasn't an act. You really didn't know?'

'Of course I didn't know,' she retorted indignantly, furious with Tony for not telling her. So that was why he was always darting off to London! Amusing himself with her or one of the nurses during the week, and going home to his wife on his free weekends.

The thought was very distasteful. She dug her teeth into her underlip, mortified that it should be Mackenzie of all people who had told her.

'I'm sorry, Jean,' he said with unexpected gentleness. 'Does it matter that much to you? Really matter?'

'I'm not in love with him, if that's what you're asking,' she said, low-voiced. 'I've only been out with him a few times, after all. But I thought we were friends, and it isn't nice when a friend—well—lets you down.'

He put a hand on her shoulder for a moment and gave it a squeeze. 'Don't upset yourself, little one. He really isn't worth it.'

She managed a rather shaky smile. 'I know. Please excuse me. I'll take your advice and go out somewhere.'

'If you go off on your own you'll only spend the afternoon brooding over Tony. I'm just off to my cottage in Shropshire. Care to come with me?'

It was a spur-of-the-moment offer, and she looked at him doubtfully. 'You don't have to feel sorry for me. Honestly, I'm all right.'

'I don't feel in the least sorry for you,' he said briskly. 'I haven't failed to notice how popular you are with men, so I doubt you'll be pining for long. Now come on, there's a good girl. I'm already later than I meant to be.'

'Well, honestly!' Jean said, making a half-hearted attempt to assert herself. 'I haven't said I'm coming yet.'

'No need. I've decided for you.' He gave her a little push in the direction of the door. 'You'd better get a sweater. We may be late back.'

He was waiting impatiently for her in the car park, and gave an approving nod when she appeared a minute or two later. 'Top marks, my dear. Most girls are incapable of getting ready quickly.'

The lunch hour was over, so traffic was light and in no time they had left Westhampton behind. Jean stared out of the window, thinking how unexpected it was to be sharing an afternoon with her formidable chief. The man might have been a thought-reader!

'Don't look so apprehensive. We're off duty. That puts us on equal terms, doesn't it?'

He gave her a smile of unexpected charm and she answered cautiously, 'Perhaps, but I'm not sure how far I'd like to put it to the test!'

At which he appeared hugely amused, though he didn't make any answer. He concentrated on driving, which he did fast but well, and only slowed down when they left the main roads and branched into a network of narrow lanes.

The countryside looked beautiful, sparkling and fresh

after several days' rain, and wilder than Jean had expected, with only the occasional farmhouse or cottage to be seen.

She leant back in her seat with a sigh of contentment. 'It's hard to believe we're only an hour's drive from Westhampton,' she murmured, and he nodded.

'I agree. There's still a lot of England that hasn't been spoilt. When I came down here from Scotland I didn't expect to find anything as good as this.'

They were climbing now, on the flank of a large hill. On one side lay open moorland and on the other farmland. He drew up in front of a white gate and had half opened his door when Jean jumped out.

She held the gate back and followed the car up a short drive to a small cottage tucked snugly into the side of the hill. It was built of the pinkish brown stone that seemed common in this part of Shropshire, with small windows and a blue front door. Jean was charmed and said so.

Mackenzie fished a key out of his pocket and unlocked the door. In the narrow hall there was an untidy jumble of wellington boots, mackintoshes and old hats.

'Make yourself at home,' he said. 'You won't mind if I get on with the garden? There are some deck chairs outside if you want to be lazy.'

Jean wondered if he was already having second thoughts about bringing her, and decided to make herself scarce.

'I don't feel lazy. I could do with a drink and then I'm going for a walk.'

When she set off a few minutes later he had already put on boots and was digging a new flower bed. In a T-shirt and jeans he looked years younger and much less forbidding. She waved a cheerful hand as she passed him and he called after her:

'Don't get lost. There's a lot of open country behind the cottage.'

She went through the gate at the side of the garden straight on to the hillside. She climbed steadily, stopping occasionally to get her breath until she reached what she had thought at first was the top. It wasn't, but she decided she had done enough on such a hot day, and flung herself down on the springy turf to enjoy the view.

Below, on the far side of the road lay a patchwork quilt of fields, and in the distance fold after fold of blue hills stretching into the distance. Jean hadn't been exaggerating when she had said she had always wanted to live in the country. She spent a couple of hours very happily, pottering on the hillside, which was quite deserted apart from two grubby small boys whom she pretended not to see tracking her. When they burst out on her with war whoops she showed suitable surprise, and fishing in her pockets, found a forgotten bar of chocolate which she offered them.

'You're nicer than the other one,' the older child commented.

Jean had a good deal of difficulty in understanding his accent. 'What other one?' she asked when she had worked it out, and he gave her an engaging gap-toothed grin.

'That horrid girl he sometimes brings. Mr Mackenzie—you know.'

'The one with fair hair?' she hazarded.

'That's right. And a snooty sorta voice.'

It sounded like Pauline! Jean laughed and turned to go.

'The dark one's nicer,' the younger boy said.

They fell into step beside her and Jean wondered just how many girls her chief had brought to the cottage. When she reached the gate she said goodbye to them, but they showed no sign of going.

'He lets us come in. He gives us tea sometimes.'

He was still hard at work. Having finished the flower bed, he was now laying flagstones at one side of the house. The boys greeted him as an old friend and he responded in kind.

'But keep out of that sand or I'll drop you in the water-butt.'

They giggled delightedly and he smiled across their heads at Jean.

'How about some tea? Think you can cope? Simon knows where things are.'

So Jean and Simon made the tea, cut the bread and butter and laid out a large fruit cake and some gingerbread, that were stored in tins in the larder. They looked home-made and so did the jam, and she wondered about the cook. Not Pauline, surely? It was hard to imagine Pauline in any sort of domestic role.

The simplest way to satisfy her curiosity was to ask, which she did as they all sat around the wooden kitchen table.

'My sister. She loves baking.'

When the boys had demolished an enormous tea they departed. 'Who are they?' Jean asked.

'They live in a cottage down the lane, two of a large family with a harassed mother and a farm labourer father. I sometimes wonder if they get enough to eat, so I encourage them to drop in.'

He passed his cup and Jean refilled it, thinking how strange it was to be sitting here, so at ease with him.

'Not bored?'

'No, of course not. It's a heavenly spot.'

'Glad you like it. I want to finish that path, then I'll be at your disposal.'

So Jean washed up and then, intrigued by the old cottage, went on a tour of inspection. There were three small bedrooms, with low ceilings and deep windows. Apart from the kitchen there was one other room downstairs, a comfortable room with shabby furniture and a stone fireplace. The alcoves on either side were filled with books and photographs of various family groups stood on the mantelpiece.

There was one of a smiling dark girl, and Jean picked it up to have a closer look. Another girl-friend? 'The dark one' the boys had mentioned? She had already noticed a framed snapshot of Pauline on a side table.

A tap on the window made her swing round a little guiltily, because she didn't wish to be thought nosey. Mackenzie signed to her to open it, and when she did so he leaned in to speak to her.

'Be a good girl and give me a hand. It's awkward using the spirit level on my own.'

She put the photograph carefully back on the mantelpiece and went out to join him. 'You didn't mind my looking round?' she asked a little shyly.

'Of course not. I told you to make yourself at home. Did you think she was pretty? The girl in the photo?' he added, when she gave him a blank look.

'Very,' she said stiffly, and he laughed and told her what he wanted her to do. After a few minutes he told her that he could manage on his own, so she went and sat on the gate that led into the field.

The sun was beginning to drop behind the hill and the shadows were lengthening. It was exquisitely peaceful, the only sound the occasional distant bleat of a sheep or the call of a bird.

Jean put an arm round the gatepost to steady herself and took a deep breath of the pure air. She was totally immersed in watching a couple of rabbits when Mackenzie spoke beside her.

'That's finished. How about a stroll down the lane? There's a pub in the village.'

She slipped nimbly from the gate. 'Could I just go and tidy up?'

'It's only a village pub. No need to fuss over your face. Besides'—he gave her a critical appraisal—'with a skin like that you don't need make-up.' He touched the tip of her nose, smiling faintly. 'Definitely shiny, but it suits you. Except that you look about sixteen and they may not allow you in the bar!'

The pub was delightful, though a trifle overcrowded. They were all local farming types, judging by their clothes, but they greeted Mackenzie as one of themselves, and towards Jean they extended a grave courtesy. They had their drinks sitting on the bench by the front door.

'If we stay inside you'll inhibit them too much,' Mackenzie smiled. 'They're not really used to women in the bar.'

She drank two ciders thirstily, because it was a warm evening, and later walking back to the cottage, she asked him how long ago he'd bought it.

'When I first came here. Like you, Jean, I always wanted to live in the country.'

'Where did you live before?' she asked, and he told her, 'Glasgow. On the fringe of one of the toughest areas in a very tough city.' She must have showed her surprise, because he went on, 'I didn't have the sort of childhood you must have had, my dear girl. My father was a brilliant engineer who became a chronic alcoholic. He lost job after job, and we sank lower and lower down the social scale as a result. My mother tried desperately to keep up some sort of standard, but she fought a losing battle. Died quite young of a coronary, brought on in my opinion by overwork and worry.'

'And your father?'

'He died at forty—a wasted life. After his death my mother went back to nursing for a few years, but she was never a strong woman.'

He sounded very bitter and Jean said hesitantly, 'Don't blame your father too much. And perhaps your mother loved him in spite of everything. After all, material standards aren't everything.'

'That platitude could only be offered by someone who's always been comfortably off,' he said sharply.

'Some platitudes are true,' she countered with equal sharpness.

They had reached the cottage and he held the gate open for her, his expression disagreeable. 'Have you any idea what it's like living with an alcoholic? No, of course you haven't. The promises of reform that mean nothing. The stealing of already inadequate housekeeping money. I can never remember my mother as anything but shabby, and she lost her looks far earlier than most women do. We never had a proper holiday in my entire childhood.'

She would have been far more sympathetic if his manner hadn't been so unpleasant. As it was she replied rather coolly, 'Are you sure your resentment isn't more on your own account because you were poor too?'

There was a flash of real anger in his eyes now. They had stopped by the front door and he stood with the key in his hand, looking down at her from his considerable height.

'Quite the little psychologist, aren't you? But you're wrong, Miss Muir, I was a tough child—I had to be, living in that area—and I didn't waste time hankering after things I couldn't have. I worked like the devil, at school and university, to get them, and I did. My one regret is that my mother didn't live long enough to share in my success.'

He put the key in the lock, opened the door and walked in ahead of her. It wasn't deliberate rudeness. He had been profoundly disturbed by his memories and had probably forgotten all about her. She felt ashamed now of her tactless remark. No, worse than tactless! Uncharitable, and untrue, because he had had a deep affection for his mother. She followed him slowly into the living-room where he was standing with one hand on the mantelpiece, staring down unseeingly at the unlit fire.

'Please don't be angry, Mr Mackenzie. I'm truly sorry if I upset you.'

He raised his head and looked at her rather blankly.

'We were having such a nice time,' she went on unhappily. 'At least,' she amended quickly, 'I was,' because he doubtless regretted that he had brought her.

Quite suddenly and unexpectedly his face softened and he smiled. 'I'm sorry too, Jean. I can't think how we got on to the subject of my family life. I don't usually indulge in bouts of self-pity. Perhaps it's because you're such a good listener.'

'Are we going back now?'

'I hadn't intended to, until we'd eaten.'

'I thought maybe you'd had enough of my company.' She gave him an uncertain half smile. 'You've been terribly kind, but——'

'I haven't been in the least kind,' he cut in abruptly. 'You were free and I was free, and it seemed a good idea to ask you.'

Strange, Jean thought, how some people hated to admit to generous impulses. 'Of course you've been kind,' she retorted. 'You thought I needed cheering up. It wouldn't have occurred to you in the normal way to invite me here, now would it?'

His eyes twinkled. 'It might have occurred to me, but I doubt I'd have done anything about it.'

'What does that mean?' Jean asked suspiciously.

'No man is averse to taking out a pretty girl,' he said blandly. 'Besides, I have a weakness for blondes, as you may have noticed.'

He was teasing her, of course, but he made her feel ridiculously shy and somehow very unsure of herself.

'Shall I get supper?' she asked, for something to say. 'What's available?'

'Bacon and eggs. Which I'll get, because you've done all the chores so far. But you could light the fire. It's getting chilly now.'

So she lit the carefully laid paper, and watched the twigs and then the logs catch fire and burn briskly. In their fine London house there was not one open fire, and Jean thought that a pity.

'We could have eaten in the kitchen,' she said, sitting

cross-legged on the hearthrug while he laid the table 'Now there'll be another grate to clean out.'

'My sister does all that,' and in answer to her questioning look, 'the one on the mantelpiece, whom you were examining so carefully.'

'Oh, honestly!' She restrained herself with an effort from saying anything more.

'Come now, Miss Muir,' he teased her, 'admit you were curious,' and he went out of the room laughing to himself.

She jumped up when the telephone rang.

'Would you answer it?' Mackenzie called from the kitchen. 'I can't leave this for a moment.'

When she gave the number a woman's voice answered. 'Is Alex there? Who's that speaking?'

'Jean Muir.' The voice sounded familiar. 'Can I give him a message?'

'No, Miss Muir. I want to speak to him.' The voice had an edge to it now, and Jean thought she recognised it.

'Hang on. It is Miss Chalmers, isn't it?'

Pauline said yes, it was, and she wanted to speak to Alex urgently, so Jean put the telephone down and went through to the kitchen.

When she gave him the message he looked faintly irritated. 'Find out what she wants. The chips will burn if I leave them.'

She removed the spatula from his hand. 'I'll carry on. Do speak to her. She sounds cross.'

He gave her a sharp look and went out, and she heard his deep voice a moment later.

'Yes, Pauline? I see. It sounds as if I'd better look at him. No, not at once. We're just about to have a meal. Oh, she was off duty, so she came with me. No, of course not. If you'll excuse me, Pauline, we are just about to eat. I'll be back at the hospital by ten-thirty.'

When he returned he was looking rather put out. Jean, carefully lifting out the chip basket, said, 'I couldn't help overhearing. Is her father not well?'

'Oh, some flap on. He probably has indigestion, but Pauline won't take the word of the nursing staff for it.'

They carried their food through to the living-room, and he ate a little absentmindedly, the frown still on his face.

'I'm sorry if my being here has made things awkward,' Jean ventured.

He shrugged. 'I shouldn't have rushed off anyway. Your being here makes no difference.'

'It might to Pauline. I mean—you know—she may not like your bringing other girls here.'

'What the devil are you talking about? I bring whom I please. It has nothing to do with Pauline.' He looked both annoyed and astonished at her suggestion. 'We're not engaged, you know.'

She glanced at Pauline's photograph. 'But you must be quite fond of her or you wouldn't have that.'

'She put it there herself,' he informed her ungallantly, and Jean thought again, 'Poor Pauline.'

'Please don't be cross,' she said quickly. 'I'm sorry if I spoke out of turn.'

He gave her a grudging smile. 'We do have a knack of rubbing each other up the wrong way. I wonder why.'

'The psychologists would call it incompatible personalities,' Jean said half jokingly, and the awkward moment passed.

When they were preparing to leave Simon and his brother appeared as from nowhere, to wave them off and shut the gate after them.

'When are your nephews coming again?' Simon asked, and Mackenzie told them, next weekend.

'Will she be coming again?' the younger boy pointed to Jean, and the surgeon aimed a playful slap at him.

'Manners, please. Her name is Miss Muir, and I doubt she'll want to come back if she has to put up with you laddies.'

They giggled, and waved energetically as the car moved off down the drive.

'Does your sister come here often? Where does she live?'

'In Birmingham, so she likes to get away to the country as frequently as possible. You must meet her some time. I think you'd get on well together. She's a nice uncomplicated sort of person.'

Which he, most definitely, was not, for the tough manner was partly a façade. He had loved his mother deeply and he was good with children. His attitude to women seemed a bit ruthless, however. It reminded her of her brother Tom's. In fact when she thought about it Tom and Alex had a good deal in common. They were both brilliant in their own specialities, ambitious, driving men who didn't suffer fools gladly. Tom was probably as difficult to work for as this man.

'You're very silent, Jean. Not wasting your thoughts on young Wilson, I hope?'

'No. No, of course not.' He looked sceptical, so she went on quickly, 'As a matter of fact I was thinking how similar you are to my brother Tom.'

'Should I be flattered by the comparison?' and when she hesitated, 'Well, come on, what's he like?'

'Very clever,' Jean said slowly. 'Um—perhaps a little hard—a bit of a materialist——'

'Well, thanks,' he said drily. 'I can see the comparison does me no credit at all. Are you fond of this clever, hard, materialistic brother of yours?'

They had grown up together, fought together, protected each other from their elders. 'Yes, of course I'm fond of him, though we do have a good many fights.'

He looked amused. 'Now I understand why you're so touchy with me. I remind you of your brother! What do you fight about?'

'Oh, anything—nothing. Sometimes he can be very unfeeling, and I wish he was a bit—well—gentler.'

'So you like gentle, idealistic men, little one?'

'Yes, I do. Like most women.'

'That seems to me a debatable point. Toughness definitely appeals to a certain type of female. But your type'—why did he have to sound so disparaging?—'tends to confuse gentleness with lack of guts! Women are so muddle-headed when it comes to their emotions!'

'You haven't much of an opinion of women, have you?'

'Not much,' he agreed. 'I can't help remembering how my popularity rating went up when I qualified! It was different when I was a poor student.'

She wondered how much justification there was for this cynical comment, and had to admit that a lot of women were out for what they could get. 'But not all,' she said earnestly. 'A girl like—well, like Liz Davies wouldn't care a hoot what a man's position in life was if she loved him.'

'A very feminine characteristic,' he said lightly, 'to argue from the general to the particular. So you admire Sister Davies, do you? So do I. An absolutely splendid girl.'

He spoke with genuine warmth, and Jean, remembering Liz's admission, wondered if there was any chance for her friend after all.

'Liz admires you too!' she blurted out, and then could have kicked herself for such a naïve remark.

'Does she indeed? So you have cosy little sessions comparing notes about your male colleagues?' he asked sarcastically. 'I hate to think what you'll say about today.'

'You've got it all wrong!' she cried. 'Liz and I don't gossip. Not in the way you mean. I wouldn't dream of passing on any of the things you've told me. And if you think I would, then you're even more—more——'

'Objectionable? Lacking in finer feelings? In sensitivity?' he supplied mockingly.

'You're quite impossible,' Jean snapped. 'And I was wrong. Compared with you Tom comes off very well indeed!' No sooner had she uttered this decidedly childish remark than she remembered with an uncomfortable jolt that the man was her superior. 'I suppose I should apologise,' she added lamely, 'but I'm beginning to think you do it on purpose. Trying to make me lose my cool.'

She risked a glance at him and was relieved to see that he was smiling broadly. 'I believe I do. You rise so beautifully. But I meant what I said. We're on equal terms when we're off duty.'

She wondered why she had ever doubted that. Whatever his faults Alexander Mackenzie was not a petty man. He steered the conversation into safe impersonal channels for the rest of the journey, and when they arrived at the hospital they walked together from the car park.

In the main hall Pauline Chalmers rose from one of the benches to meet them. She ignored Jean completely, putting a hand on Mackenzie's arm, and looking up at him with wide anxious eyes.

'I've been so worried, Alex.' There was a hint of reproach in her voice. 'Thank goodness you're here at last!'

'I'm sure you've been worrying unnecessarily, my dear. I saw your father this morning before I left for the cottage.'

'Perhaps I have,' she agreed softly. 'But I feel happier now you're back.'

She kept her hand on his arm as they turned towards the lift, and Jean, who hadn't had a chance to thank him, lingered in the hall for a moment, looking after them. He turned to smile at her, and raised a hand in farewell, so she called out, 'Good night, Mr Mackenzie, and thank you for the outing.'

The lift doors clanged shut on her last words, but not before she had caught the fleeting expression of anger on Pauline's face.

It amused Jean because it was so unnecessary. The idea that Pauline could look on her as a possible rival was quite ridiculous. He regarded her as a tiresome, argumentative girl, which she seemed to become in his company. Jean, who was usually easy-going and tolerant, brooded on the reason for this as she climbed the stairs to her bedroom.

All that fresh air and sunshine had made her very sleepy, so she thought she would skip the usual nightcap in Sister's office. Besides, Tony would almost certainly be there, and she didn't feel like meeting him just yet. She had spoken the truth to Alex. She wasn't the least bit in love with Tony, but his deception rankled. She wasn't good at putting on an act, wouldn't feel at ease with him again until she had talked to him in private.

Her last thoughts, though, before she drifted off to sleep, weren't of Tony but of Alex. He had been a tough little boy in a tough city, but perhaps he had been more vulnerable than the grown man remembered. The family group on the cottage mantelpiece had shown a sturdy determined child, but there was also a wistfulness about the young face, that could indicate his awareness of family tensions.

Early childhood was said to condition one's character for life. The hard streak in his nature, that she had found unattractive on occasion, might not have been there if he had had a different upbringing.

## CHAPTER SEVEN

'MY word!' commented Peter, after Thursday's operating session, 'the big chief has mellowed! Especially towards you.'

'He does seem to be less critical,' Jean agreed. 'Let's hope it lasts.'

A vain hope, however, as next day's fracture clinic proved. Fracture clinics were always busy and often gruelling. Seventy to eighty patients came and went in the space of three hours, wheeled in by the nurses, hobbling on crutches, walking if they could, the whole supervised in a masterly fashion by the Outpatient Sister, a calm intelligent woman who got on splendidly with Mr Mackenzie. She was the only member of the nursing staff Jean had ever heard answer him back, though she did it so politely he couldn't possibly take offence.

Halfway through the morning she announced that it was time for a short break.

Mackenzie swivelled round in his chair, to dictate a note to his secretary, sitting just behind him. 'Later, Sister. We're already behind time.'

'Then an extra five minutes can't matter,' Sister said firmly, signalling to the junior nurse who hovered in the doorway with the coffee tray.

'I'm thinking of the patients,' he said irritably, giving the poor girl a ferocious glare as she knocked over a pile of notes in trying to make room for the tray.

'I'm thinking of the patients too,' Sister replied. 'I can tell to the nearest half hour, sir, when your blood sugar is beginning to drop.'

For a moment he looked annoyed, then he gave a reluctant smile. 'Are you telling me I've been bad-tempered this morning, Sister?'

'A little ... hasty, perhaps, sir. You've had two of my nurses in tears and poor Dr Muir run off her feet trying to keep up with you.'

'Good for her,' he said unfeelingly, but he beckoned Jean forward. 'Sit down, Miss Muir, while you can. Do you think I'm a slavedriver?'

Jean made a noncommittal reply and Pollock, who helped run the fracture clinic, said thoughtfully, 'Patients must often feel very critical of us. There they are, a seemingly endless line outside the clinic, and they see a nurse bringing in our mid-mornings. But Sister's right, we do need a break or our efficiency suffers.'

Jean nodded her agreement. Even in her relatively minor role she felt drained after a busy clinic. Medicine was emotionally as well as physically taxing. The best of her teachers had constantly stressed the need for doctors to be tolerant towards their patients, even when they were at their most demanding. The reverse was also true, however. Patients ought to make more allowances for their doctors, might do so more often if they realised that an irritable doctor was possibly a tired doctor.

'We could do with a public relations man in every hospital,' she suggested, 'trying to improve the doctor–patient relationship.'

'They have them in America,' said Pollock.

'God forbid,' Mackenzie growled. 'Just one more way of diverting limited money from where it's really needed. And there's nothing wrong with your doctor–patient relationship, Miss Muir. If you can handle Sefton Chalmers you can handle anybody! Which reminds me, he's grumbling because you haven't been to see him. Says he asked you to go.'

'Oh,' Jean said, faintly surprised, 'I didn't think he really meant it.'

He drained the last of his coffee and stood up. 'Sefton

never says what he doesn't mean. So look in on him this evening, there's a good girl. Is that child with the fractured femur out of plaster yet, Sister?'

Even the private patients ate at the ridiculously early time of six o'clock. Jean reckoned that Mr Chalmers should have finished his supper by six-thirty, so as she had a rare half hour free, she went along to see him.

He was stirring his coffee and looked rather bad-tempered.

'No need to wait, Staff,' Jean said to the nurse. 'This is a social call,' and to Mr Chalmers, 'Have I picked an inconvenient time?' She smiled at him and although he didn't return the smile his scowl vanished.

'The food is absolutely terrible,' he grunted, 'and the coffee's undrinkable. I swear my indigestion's worse since I've been in here. Well, sit down, sit down, don't hover in the doorway like that.'

Jean smiled more broadly and sat down by his bed. 'Your food can't be that bad, Mr Chalmers. The doctors eat the same as the ward patients. I wouldn't say it's exciting, but it's quite adequate. And yours is bound to be better than ours as you're a private patient.'

'Adequate,' he grumbled. 'Food should be more than adequate. Are you telling me I'm making a fuss, young woman?'

He looked tired and irritable, and moved restlessly in his bed as if he couldn't get comfortable. Jean had found that the rich seldom made as good patients as the poor. No hospital, however good, could come up to the home standards of a wealthy man.

'Not exactly making a fuss, but perhaps expecting too much. They try awfully hard in the kitchens on a very limited catering allowance. Let me prop you up a bit, then you'll feel more comfortable.'

When she had helped him he managed a brief smile. She had an idea that smiling didn't come easily to him, perhaps from lack of practice.

'I've had a devil of a day,' he confessed. 'First Alex tells me that I shall be in longer than I expected. Then my fool of a secretary makes a complete muck-up of some important letters. She was highly recommended, but she seems incapable of rational thought.'

'Perhaps you frighten her so much she can't think straight,' she suggested.

'Frighten her? Do I frighten you?'

'No, but I don't work for you.' She added softly, 'Thank goodness,' but took the sting out of her words by the charm of her smile.

Sefton Chalmers gave a barking laugh. 'Haven't much opinion of me, have you, young woman? I suppose you only came to see me because you were sorry for me, eh?' He accompanied this with such a ferocious look that Jean began to giggle.

When she could control herself she gasped, 'I came because Mr Mackenzie asked me. I'd have come before, but I didn't think you really wanted to see me. And if you glare at your secretary like that I'm surprised that she doesn't hand in her notice.'

'Not enough gumption for it! Besides, I pay her damned well.'

He probably had to or he wouldn't keep her. Jean said earnestly, 'There's a stage in every patient's convalescence when nothing seems right. It's a good sign in a way. It means you're on the mend.' She laid her small hand lightly over his. 'You've had a tough time, Mr Chalmers, but at least you're alive, unlike your unfortunate chauffeur.'

There was an odd expression on his face as he looked down at her hand. 'You really care about people, don't you, my dear? Is that what made you take up medicine?'

'I wanted to do something worthwhile,' Jean admitted, 'and coming from a medical family it seemed the obvious choice.' She turned his hand over gently. 'It's healed well, hasn't it? I'm glad.'

The scar on his palm was surprisingly neat, though the stitch holes still showed.

'What a touching scene,' said Sefton's daughter. 'Fortunate I'm not Mother!'

Jean turned to look at Pauline, who must have come in very quietly. The words were malicious, and her expression even more so.

Sefton went an alarming brick red, but with anger rather than embarrassment. 'Don't be more of a fool than you must be,' he rasped. 'You know perfectly well Miss Muir's a doctor. As she sewed my hand up—and very well too, according to Alex—she was naturally interested in how it was doing.'

Pauline's colour had risen too. 'Can't you take a joke, darling?' But there wasn't much warmth in the endearment. She threw her cream suede jacket down on the end of the bed, and settled herself in the armchair by the window.

'Seeing how Dr Muir wasn't wearing her white coat for once, I didn't realise this was a duty call.'

Jean stood up, determined not to let the girl's manner provoke her. 'I really must go, Mr Chalmers. First come, first served in our mess, and it's just on suppertime.'

She gave Pauline a polite nod and moved towards the door.

'Come again,' said Sefton. 'You cheer me up, my dear.'

Pauline looked the other way.

Jean went down to supper, more ruffled by this episode than she realised, which made her less inclined to join in the lighthearted banter round the table than she usually was.

Tony, sitting on her left, finished telling a funny story about one of the patients, and under cover of the general laughter put his head close to hers.

'What's up? You look very glum tonight.'

'I don't think jokes about patients are funny,' Jean said

stiffly.

He gave her an incredulous look. 'This one was,' and of course he was right. It had been funny, without being unkind. Usually she would have laughed as much as the others. In hospital if you didn't keep a sense of humour, the sad side of your work, the medical battles that were lost instead of won, could become almost unbearable.

'Something's on your mind,' Tony went on. 'For that matter you've been giving me the brush-off for the last two days. I wonder why?'

'I don't want to talk about it here,' Jean said, low-voiced, 'but if you can spare five minutes come up to my room after supper.'

She was so thoroughly out of temper anyway that she felt just in the mood to speak her mind to Tony. When he rapped on her door she was sitting by the window, putting a few stitches in a dropped hem.

'Very domesticated,' he grinned. 'I can just see you in a year or two, darning your old man's socks.'

That gave her an easy opening. Jean put her sewing down and looked at him steadily. 'Does your wife darn your socks, Tony?'

He gaped at her, for once not ready with a quick come-back.

'Why didn't you tell me you were married?'

Into the lengthening uncomfortable silence he said sulkily, 'You never asked me. It didn't seem important.'

'It obviously isn't important to you,' Jean said scornfully. 'But it presumably is to your wife, and it certainly is to me. I don't go around with married men.'

Tony walked up and down the room restlessly, and came back to her side. 'Don't make a big thing out of it. All I did was kiss you a few times. And anyway, Barbara and I—we've more or less broken up.'

'That doesn't surprise me. I suppose she couldn't take your philandering any more. And I'm not making a scene.

Why should I? Only it's left a bad taste in my mouth because I thought we were friends.'

He had the grace to look a little ashamed then. 'I suppose I should have got around to telling you sooner. For that matter, who did?'

'Mr Mackenzie.'

'Now why should he do a sneaky thing like that?' Tony asked softly. 'And how the heck did he know anyway?'

So Jean told him briefly just what had happened. 'And if he hadn't been so extraordinarily nice about it I'd have felt even worse than I did,' she ended. 'It made me look such a fool. Though I did manage to convince him that I'm not so idiotic as to get in too deep with a dubious character like you.'

'Well, thanks for those kind words,' Tony said sarcastically. 'And why was it important to convince him of that?'

Why indeed? But it had been. Jean said a little confusedly, 'Because he's the sort of man who doesn't cheat other people, I suppose. Because I didn't like him having a bad opinion of me, especially when it was unjustified.'

'Because he's the big chief, more likely,' Tony said cynically. 'Or perhaps you're thinking of making a play for him? Quite a feather in your cap, that would be, if the high and mighty Alex fell for his little house surgeon.'

Jean really blew up at that. She told Tony very plainly what she thought of his cheap flippant jokes. In fact she worked herself into such a temper that when the telephone rang it scarcely registered with her.

Tony, looking glad of a respite, snatched it up. 'For you,' he said, and made his escape while Jean was coping with the problem of how to fit two new emergency patients into an already overcrowded ward. By the time she had sorted this out she had completely cooled down, and felt indeed rather ashamed of her outburst.

Tony's flippant remark had hardly merited such a violent response, and if he had coupled her name with anyone but

Mackenzie's she would probably have laughed it off. It was the sort of rather silly teasing she should be used to by now, and after five years in medical school and nine months as a hospital resident, she had learnt to accept the fact that life in a closed community allowed one very little privacy.

That was why their free time was so treasured, and Jean, a bit jaded by the past two weeks, was more than usually glad that tomorrow was Saturday and her weekend off.

She was away just after nine in the morning, and at her London home by midday, but was a little downcast to find that none of her family were in. Lise, the Swiss housekeeper who had been with them as long as Jean could remember, said that her mother would be back soon.

'Sit on the terrace and I will bring you a nice lemon drink. You look tired, and no wonder. All that driving, and that so unsuitable work!' By which Lise meant unsuitable for a woman, and in her opinion unnecessary for a girl who came from a background like Jean's. 'If you must do this doctoring,' she continued, when she returned with the lemon drink, 'could it not be in London, so that your poor parents could see more of you, their only daughter?'

Lise was given to over-dramatising, and her heavily accented English magnified this trait. Jean, sucking gratefully on a straw, found this very funny.

'Oh, come off it, Lise dear. Can you see Mum and Dad in the role of pathetic neglected parents? They're both so busy they hardly notice we're around.'

'Of course they do,' Lise said firmly. 'The Frau Doktor is very involved with her work, naturally, because it is so important, but she always has time for the problems of her children.'

Jean didn't entirely agree with this. She adored her brilliant, witty mother, who managed to combine the role of wife to a leading academic with her own distinguished career as a biochemist. However, she couldn't remember any time, even when she was very little, when her mother had really listened to her. It was Lise who had been the comforter, and to a lesser extent her father.

'Why do you approve of Mother's career but not of mine?' she asked, putting down the glass, and stretching out on the comfortable lounger.

The midday sun was hot on her face, and she shut her eyes and waited for Lise's reply. 'Because your mother is who she is and you are you.'

'That's no sort of answer,' Jean said lazily, and Lise added by way of explanation, 'The Frau Doktor is much stronger than you, little one. What you call nowadays tough. Yes, tougher than most men, though she looks so feminine. But you, you are not tough at all. You are the soft one of the family. Perhaps it is because you are the youngest and the only girl.'

She smiled very sweetly at Jean and picked up the glass. 'I must prepare the lunch. You will have it out here, yes? It is such a lovely day.'

So Jean lay back and looked through half-closed eyes at the sundial at the end of the terrace and the walled garden beyond. Since she had last been home someone had bought more tubs, and filled them with dainty little conifers and masses of bright annuals. Instant gardening, money no object! Lise almost certainly, because no one else would have the time or the interest, and gardeners were virtually unobtainable in central London.

Dr Muir had a beautiful home, which she took for granted. She was inclined to take Lise for granted too, because Lise never complained.

'I don't want to become like Mother,' Jean thought, 'letting other people run my house and bring up my children.'

Perhaps Lise was right and she wasn't cut out to be a career woman, and yet she loved her work and knew, without being conceited, that she was good at it.

'Do you think I'm soft?' she asked her mother that evening when the two of them were alone in the drawing-room. 'Lise says I am.'

Joanna Muir, tall, good-looking and extremely elegant, flicked an amused glance at her young daughter's face.

'Yes, of course, darling, but in an attractive sort of way. You're the kind of girl everyone helps, which I never was.'

'For soft read dim, I suppose,' Jean said with a sigh. 'At least, by the standards of our family.'

'Nonsense,' Dr Muir said briskly. 'Your academic record was very good, if not as outstanding as the boys'. Why all this soul-searching anyway?'

'Oh, I don't know. Now and then I wonder if I'm in the wrong job.'

'Of course you're not. Gentle, kindly people are needed in medicine. I should have been a hopeless physician, no good at tolerating fools.'

Lack of tolerance might be said to be a family failing, or perhaps impatience with less gifted people was a better way of putting it. Intellectual arrogance, in short. Jean, who had struggled through Physics and Chemistry for her pre-medical exams, had always envied her brothers' more scientific brains.

Her youngest brother Tom, who had been going through a phase of 'be nice to Jean' at that time, had helped her a great deal. He was away this weekend and only turned up a short time before she was due to leave on the Sunday evening.

'Has Mother told you I'll be in Westhampton at the end of the month?' he asked, lounging on her bed while she collected the few belongings she wanted to take back. 'I'm giving some postgraduate lectures on Computers in Medicine. We wanted to hold them in Manchester, but it clashed with some other conference. I believe you've got quite a decent little postgrad centre at Westhampton?'

In fact it had been built only three years ago, financed entirely by private subscriptions, mainly from the big industrial firms. Sefton Chalmers, Jean knew, had donated some staggering sum.

'Don't be so patronising,' she retorted, throwing a cushion at his head. 'It's a super modern building, and we have some excellent meetings in it.'

A grin appeared on her brother's thin intelligent face. 'You really have a thing about Westhampton, don't you? I'm curious to see what it is that attracts you to the place.'

## CHAPTER EIGHT

JUNE seemed hardly to have come in before it was nearly over. The Trauma Unit was, as always, hectically busy, but although she worked very hard Jean found life a good deal easier, because of Mr Mackenzie's changed attitude towards her. He was less critical and more friendly, though he didn't again invite her to the cottage.

That was hardly to be expected because consultants didn't usually hobnob with their juniors. However, once or twice when she had a free afternoon, Jean thought a little wistfully that she would have liked to be asked.

Sir Geoffrey, fully recovered, went home with strict instructions to take life very easily. Sefton Chalmers, who knew him slightly, said, 'Lucky devil! This inactivity is driving me crazy.'

Jean, who visited him regularly now, told him to simmer down or he would end with a coronary himself. A curious relationship had been established between them. In the residents' mess they ribbed her and talked about her sugar-daddy, but Jean only smiled and let it pass because she knew it wasn't like that.

'I wish I'd had a daughter like you,' Sefton said one day, 'but I suppose it's my fault Pauline is the way she is, spoilt and shallow.'

He lapsed into moody silence, and Jean tried to cheer him up. 'I know she's rather self-centred, but she'll grow up some day.'

'Grow up?' he grunted. 'She's a year older than you are. No, she won't change. She's like her mother, a self-indulgent snob.' There was bitterness in his voice, as well there might be, because Jean knew that his wife rarely visited him.

She had met Mrs Chalmers briefly once and had not taken to her—a handsome blonde, a good deal younger than her husband, with a synthetic smile and a hard voice.

'I have no illusions about my womenfolk,' he went on bleakly. 'My wife married me for what I could give her, and considered it a fair bargain because she was better born than me.'

'I don't think you ought to tell me these things,' Jean demurred. 'You might regret it later.'

'Why should I? You're a doctor and wouldn't betray confidences. Lying here, unable to sleep, I've thought a lot about the past and the mistakes I've made. When I was around thirty there were two girls in my life. One had looks and breeding and the other had neither. She was just an ordinary girl, but she loved me, and I let her down. I picked my wife for her social assets, which just shows I'm not as smart as I like to think.'

This sort of brooding over the past was very common in those who had been seriously ill. Jean had indeed listened to many variations on this theme, and she knew it often helped to talk to a sympathetic outsider.

'You've always been so busy making money,' she suggested, 'that you haven't felt the need for a close relationship with your wife or daughter. So perhaps they thought you didn't want it. If you showed them that you did need them after all....' Her voice tailed away beneath his sceptical look.

'It's years too late for that, my dear child, but we've talked enough about my affairs. Tell me what you've been doing.'

He liked to hear about her work, and she gave him strictly edited versions of some of her cases. He took a keen interest in the young doctors too, and their living conditions.

'I want to make some sort of thank-you present when I leave. You're tied to the hospital for such long hours. When you're on call, but not actually working, how do you pass the time?'

'We play cards or chess or watch TV. We've often thought it would be nice if we had our own table tennis outfit, instead of having to share the nurses'. If you really mean it, Mr Chalmers, we'd be very grateful for one.'

He dismissed this suggestion with a scornful wave of his hand. 'I'd thought of something better than that. Haven't got a swimming pool, have you?'

Jean stared at him. 'But that would be fabulously expensive, surely?'

He didn't bother to answer this. 'But would you like one? Under cover, I think, and heated, then you could use it all the year round. And the nurses too, don't you agree?'

Jean did agree, still rather bemused by the casual way he could talk about a present of such magnitude. He was just telling her of a firm who specialised in building swimming pools, when Alexander Mackenzie came in, alone.

'A timely arrival, Alex. Jean and I have decided that the residents could do with a swimming pool, and I plan to build one. Quite an idea, eh?'

Alex's eyebrows shot up. 'Quite an idea,' he concurred, stressing the last word, 'but not exactly practical, Sefton. Where would you put it, for example? The few open spaces in the hospital grounds are already being gobbled up by ward extensions and such like.'

'It would need a little planning,' Sefton admitted, not a whit put out by the surgeon's dry tone. 'But I'm dead serious, and I usually get what I want.'

'In our affairs it's what the Hospital Management Committee wants,' Mackenzie reminded him rather coolly. 'You may be the kingpin of your business empire, but here you're just another patient.'

Mr Chalmers' temper, never very reliable, showed signs of wearing thin. 'Good grief, man, I'm only trying to show my appreciation to you all. What an arrogant bunch you medical men are!'

Which was the pot calling the kettle black with a vengeance. However, Jean had to agree that her chief did seem to be making an ungracious response to a staggeringly generous offer.

'I'd better go,' she murmured, and Mackenzie gave a curt nod. 'I think you had, Miss Muir, but wait for me in my office, please. I have something to say to you.'

She waited uneasily, at a loss to understand how she could have annoyed him. When he arrived a few minutes later he waved her into a chair, and seated himself at the desk.

'I should have thought, after the episode with young Wilson, you might have learnt some discretion,' he began. 'Pauline is so upset by your behaviour that she asked me to speak to you, since she knew you wouldn't listen to her.'

'About what?' Jean asked, searching her mind for anything that could have offended Pauline recently.

'Don't play the innocent, my girl! You know perfectly well what I'm speaking about. Your relationship with Sefton.'

After a moment of disbelief Jean reacted violently. 'Oh, honestly! What absolute rubbish! I visit the man a few times—at your request, if you remember—and Pauline makes a big thing out of it. Does she think I've fallen for him? Well, you can tell her I don't go for older men.'

'But Sefton goes for young girls,' he replied coldly. 'The man's notorious, and you've been encouraging him.'

'I have not!'

'Pauline says she found you holding hands one day.'

If the subject hadn't been so distasteful it would have been ludicrous. Torn between anger at Pauline's spitefulness and a slightly hysterical desire to laugh, Jean tried to explain the episode, but somewhow it sounded rather lame, and under his sceptical gaze she found herself stammering. Flustered, she ended defiantly. 'If you must know, I think of him like—well, like an uncle.'

'I doubt that Sefton thinks of you like a niece,' he observed sarcastically. 'When Pauline tackled me a few days ago I was inclined to think she was exaggerating, but after what I've just heard I've changed my mind. If you were a plain girl instead of a very pretty one, do you think Sefton would want to build a swimming pool for you?'

'Not for me. For us all.'

'But at your suggestion, you little fool, and I shudder to think what the gossips could make of that.'

'It was not my suggestion. It was his.'

'But you jumped at the idea, and encouraged by your approval it will doubtless be something more personal next time. Jewellery, perhaps.'

'It's not like that,' Jean said obstinately, 'and Pauline must know it. She's trying to make trouble because she doesn't like me.'

His mouth thinned ominously. 'Leave Pauline out of it, please. I think it's you who're the trouble-maker, Miss Muir. What I can't decide is whether you're just incredibly naïve or the sort of girl who gets a kick out of seeing a man make an idiot out of himself.'

So he had her cast as either a fool or a villain! And neither was justified. Her relationship with Sefton, disagreeable expression, was what it seemed on the surface, she was absolutely sure of that.

'You're being very unfair,' she said helplessly.

She might not have spoken for all the attention he paid her. 'On the whole I'll give you the benefit of the doubt. I suppose you've traded on your feminine charm for so long that you don't even realise you're doing it.'

She flushed angrily and jumped to her feet. 'Since you won't listen to me I might as well go!'

For a big man he could move surprisingly quickly. He was at the door before she was, blocking her way out. 'I haven't finished yet,' he said softly. He put his hands on her shoulders and shook her, none too gently. 'Stay away from Sefton, Miss Muir. Do you understand?'

The small room seemed to intensify their closeness, and their hostility. Jean's heart began to hammer in a most disturbing way. Her voice came out rather huskily. 'I don't think you have any control over what I do off duty. If I visit Mr Chalmers as a friend you have no right to stop me.'

'I may not have the right, but I'll do it just the same,' he promised grimly. 'If you visit Sefton I'll make your life on the Trauma Unit so disagreeable you'll wonder what's hit you. I'm not making idle threats and you know it.'

She did know it, because he was in a position to carry out his threat, and ruthless enough to do it.

'You're being very unfair,' she said again, and humiliatingly her eyes filled with tears.

He gave an unkind laugh. 'Crying because you can't have your own way?' and then as the tears spilled over, 'Oh, for God's sake, girl, wipe your eyes. I can't stand women who cry.'

She fumbled vainly for a handkerchief, furious with herself for such loss of control, and he muttered something under his breath and produced a handkerchief from his pocket.

'What a child you are in some ways! I suppose I shouldn't lose my temper with you——' he put hard fingers under her chin and forced her to look up at him, scrubbing her cheeks briskly, as if she really was the child he had called her. 'Stop looking at me like that,' he said roughly, and his hand stilled for a moment inches away from her face.

There was something electric between them, an intense awareness of each other, a physical thing felt by them both. She knew it by his expression. Panicking, she wrenched herself out of his grasp and backed away across the small room.

'What did you think I was going to do?' he jeered. 'Kiss you? I feel more like shaking you till your teeth rattle!' He flung the door open and made an impatient gesture of dismissal. 'You'd better go, Miss Muir, before I do just that.'

She walked down the corridor on unsteady legs, thinking that she disliked him more than anyone she had ever met. He was sarcastic, unreasonable, prejudiced, lacking even in a sense of humour or he would have seen the absurdity of his accusation. He was also a bully. She almost managed to convince herself that it was fear she had experienced when he had put his hands on her. Almost, but not quite, because she was an honest girl.

She vowed to keep out of his way as much as possible, and never, never to give him the chance to humiliate her again. She only had two months left on the Trauma Unit, and she was determined to stick it out somehow. Pride would prevent her giving in her notice, quite apart from the fact that it wouldn't do her career any good.

Because she knew Mackenzie was a man who meant what he said, she stopped visiting Mr Chalmers, but after three days he sent her a message through Liz.

'He knows you're terribly busy, but he would like to see you.'

'I can't go,' Jean said flatly, and then, since Liz was her friend, 'It's laughable, I know, but his charming daughter has got it into her head that I'm after the old man.'

Liz was inclined to laugh at first, but when she had listened to Jean's story she became very thoughtful. 'The thing is, Jean, he does have a bad reputation with women, and he isn't really old, so I suppose Mackenzie was right to warn you. And even if there's nothing in it, if Pauline thinks there is she'll talk, which could be unpleasant for you. Write him a tactful note and try to explain.'

Easier said than done. Jean tore up several attempts at half-truths and in the end decided that if she said anything she had to be honest.

'Dear Mr Chalmers,' she wrote, 'I'm very sorry, but I shan't be able to visit you any more. It's quite ridiculous, but people are implying that we're interested in each other in more than just a friendly way. So for both our sakes I'd better stop seeing you, though I shall miss our chats.' She added a P.S. 'Try and see the funny side, and don't be cross.'

A vain plea, however. That evening when she was sitting in her bedroom, catching up on her correspondence, the telephone rang. Mr Chalmers had a telephone by his bed and made calls whenever he wanted.

'I've had your letter,' he growled, 'and I don't think there is a funny side. Who's been making trouble? I want to know, Jean.'

She refused to tell him, but Sefton was a shrewd man. 'Not the nurses,' he brooded. 'They'd have more sense. And my wife wouldn't care enough, so that leaves Pauline. Just the sort of silly spiteful thing she'd enjoy doing. Ignore it, my dear, and come and see me tomorrow.'

'Mr Chalmers, I really can't. Life would be too unpleasant if I did.'

'Pauline can't do anything——' he paused and gave an incredulous grunt. 'Has that daughter of mine been making trouble with Alex?' She was silent and he swore furiously. 'I'm sorry, my dear. This is worse than I realised. But I'll put things right, I promise. When I've finished with Pauline that young woman is going to be very sorry for herself. And as for Alex, I thought he had more sense!'

What was said between the two men Jean could only imagine, but at the end of their next operating session Mackenzie stopped her as she was leaving Theatre.

'Just a moment, Miss Muir.' He beckoned her into a corner, out of earshot of the nurses. 'So you've stopped seeing Sefton? Very prudent of you.'

She still had her theatre garb on and she glared at him over the top of her mask.

He laughed and tweaked it off. 'Don't look at me like that, my girl! They call it dumb insolence in the Army.'

Determined not to lose her temper, she looked down at her theatre boots and kept quiet, hoping he would go away.

'Lost your tongue, little Miss Muir?' he jeered, and she forgot all her good resolves and flashed back at him,

'I am not little! I'm quite tall for a girl, though I know you only say it to put me in my place.'

'And what is your place?'

'You know very well. I'm only a house surgeon, and you're a consultant. So I can't say what I'd like to about this whole silly business. I just have to put up with your—your dictatorial behaviour—but I hope Mr Chalmers told you what he thought of you!'

'Oh, he did, my dear girl, he did indeed.' The fact that he looked amused rather than angry only increased her exasperation. 'I hesitate to repeat what he said to a lady, but he didn't entirely convince me that his intentions were innocent.'

The cynical dark eyes mocked her and it was then that Jean lost control of her temper, and with it all restraint. 'You're the most hateful man I've ever known! You twist a decent thing like friendship so that it comes out as something unpleasant and—and furtive. I could almost feel sorry for you, having such an ungenerous, suspicious mind, except that I dislike you too much. And if you want to give me the sack for speaking the truth, then go ahead and do so!'

She delivered this impassioned speech under her breath, but with considerable force just the same. It wiped the amusement off his face, but she was still too angry to be alarmed by his grim expression. 'It would be no more than you deserve if I took you at your word,' he said bitingly. 'But I'll overlook it this time, because in spite of what you think of me, I am not a man who takes advantage of his position. Especially when dealing with someone as childishly immature as you,' and on these words he swung on his heel and left her.

There were one or two junior nurses hovering around, armed with buckets and mops to wash over the tiled floor. It was unlikely they had heard this interchange, but they had eyes in their heads and must have realised that Jean and her chief were not engaged in friendly conversation.

She changed and went along to the wards to look up the post-operative patients, but for once her mind was not entirely on her work. It had been a lamentable mistake to lose her temper. Even if Mackenzie intended no drastic action, her rash words couldn't have done her career any good. A young doctor who got a reputation as a troublemaker might find it difficult to get another post.

Miserably aware that she had been extremely foolish, she felt the urge to unburden herself to somebody. Peter was in his room, his lanky form stretched out on the bed, recovering from their long stint in Theatre. She told him what had happened and he looked unusually serious.

'You must have been mad to shoot your mouth like that! And to Alex of all people. You're darned lucky he didn't take you at your word and report you to the Hospital Management Committee. Which would almost certainly have meant the sack. But you can't expect a good reference when you leave, and that could be disastrous. Unless you apologise, that is.'

'No,' Jean said flatly. 'It's he who ought to apologise to me.'

'Oh, be your age! He's not the type who apologises. Besides, it's you who're in the wrong.'

'Well, thanks for nothing,' Jean said crossly. 'I thought you were my friend.'

Peter sat up quickly and swung his feet to the floor. 'I am, Jean, but you've got to learn the facts of life. And one of them is that you can't take on your superiors and hope to win. Ask Liz if you don't believe me.'

Liz said the same, even more forcefully.

'Swallow your pride, Jean, and apologise. I know you've never liked him, but he's fair-minded. He'll probably meet you halfway, because he was, in a sense, in the wrong too.'

Jean pounced on that. 'So you admit that, unlike Peter?'

'He accepted Pauline's word too readily,' Liz said in her calm way. 'And it sounds as if he was trying to get a rise out of you in Theatre. The thing is, Jean, you're so prickly with him. If you'd learn to laugh it off he wouldn't do it.'

'He called me immature and childish,' Jean said resentfully.

'Well, so you have been,' and when Jean tried, angrily, to interrupt, she put a hand gently but firmly across her friend's mouth. 'Listen to me! I'm fond of you and I'm trying to help. You have been rather childish, and that's not like you. It seems to me you've let your dislike of Mackenzie get quite out of hand, until you've lost all sense of proportion. You get on splendidly with everyone else. Have you ever asked yourself why you can't do the same with him?'

Jean sighed and avoided Liz's eyes. 'I suppose I don't go for big bossy men,' but even to her own ears it sounded an inadequate explanation.

Liz's voice was a little dry. 'I'm not asking you to like him—just to tolerate him, since you have to work with him. So don't you think you could take back some of those nasty things you said?'

'He would know I wasn't being sincere,' Jean muttered.

'You don't have to go into details. Just say you're sorry you lost your temper. You could do it right now.' She picked up the telephone by Jean's bed. 'Go on, ring his office. He stays late on Mondays doing research. Extension 99.'

'Well, honestly——'

'It would clear the air,' Liz insisted, her expression very serious, and her nice brown eyes anxious. 'It'll get harder to do the longer you wait.'

Jean knew in her heart that it was the sensible thing to do. She swallowed hard and took the telephone from Liz. Mackenzie's voice, when he answered, sounded rather jaded.

She stammered out a request to see him, and he said curtly, 'Oh, it's you, Miss Muir. Can't it wait till morning?'

Liz, who was close enough to hear, shook her head violently, and Jean, with a sinking heart, said that she would prefer to come this evening.

'All right!' he snapped. 'Come straight away, then,' and the telephone clicked.

When she reached his office she stood for a minute or so, staring at the name plate on his door, and feeling rather as she'd done while waiting to face the examiners in her medical finals.

'This is getting to be a habit,' she thought disconsolately, and raised her hand to knock. He looked up as she came in, his expression decidedly irritable.

'I don't know why you have to bother me. Surely one of the registrars is around?'

'It's—not to do with work,' she brought out a little huskily, and then, because her legs felt unpleasantly shaky, 'M-may I sit down?'

He ignored that, his face a blend of fatigue and ill-temper. 'Miss Muir, I have just about had my fill for today.' He let out a long breath and tipped his chair back. 'I don't feel up to any more emotional scenes, so please go away.'

'I will in a moment, truly, but I came to—to apologise. I lost my temper and said some—some very rude and disagreeable things.' The last words came out in a rush, and even though he hadn't invited her to do so, she sat down opposite the desk, and looked at him anxiously.

He had listened to this with his eyes shut, but now he opened them again, and stared at her with disconcerting intentness.

'Second thoughts, Miss Muir?' he jibed unpleasantly. 'There are some things better left unsaid, aren't there?'

So he wasn't going to meet her halfway. Perhaps, after what she had called him, that was too much to expect.

'I told Liz it was a waste of time,' she sighed, and made to rise.

'Liz? Sister Davies? This was her idea?'

'Yes. And Peter's. But—but my apology is quite sincere,' she said breathlessly. 'I was rude. I spoke in the heat of the moment, though I suppose that's no excuse.'

He passed a hand slowly over his face, and when he took it away his expression had altered and softened. 'All right, Miss Muir, I believe you. And I suppose I was at fault too for needling you unnecessarily. Do you think, if we both made a great effort, we might avoid rubbing each other up the wrong way?'

She nodded, too surprised to say anything.

'I don't particularly enjoy rows,' he went on. 'Bad for morale on the Unit. Makes us less efficient as a team.'

He rose and she took this as dismissal, and got to her feet. He walked round the desk and stood looking down at her, the hint of a smile at the corners of his mouth.

'It must have taken quite a lot of courage to come and see me.' He put his hand lightly on her shoulder. 'You look tired, little one. You're off duty, aren't you? Have an early night.'

The smile was fully in evidence now, and remarkably attractive. Jean thought a little confusedly that this must be the face he presented to his friends. Confusedly, because she was overcome again by the same rather frightening feeling that she had experienced last time she was alone with him.

She made a noncommittal reply and left, and did indeed take his advice and go to bed early.

Tired though she was, however, she found it difficult to

sleep. Physical attraction was an odd, disturbing thing, and could occur between two people who had nothing else in common. Physical attraction wasn't love, though it was often difficult to distinguish one from the other. On this disquieting thought she drifted off finally into a restless and unrefreshing sleep.

# CHAPTER NINE

BECAUSE she had had a bad night Jean was reluctant to get up in the morning, but thoughts of the fracture clinic drove her from her bed. She rushed down to breakfast to find Peter finishing his coffee.

'Get a move on,' he said. 'The boss is always there spot on nine.' Halfway to the door he swung round to ask her if it wasn't today that her brother Tom arrived.

'No, tomorrow, the twenty-ninth,' said Jean, and took a piece of toast, resigned to the fact that she had no time for anything more sustaining.

'Today is the twenty-ninth. Get with it, girl! You're half asleep!'

That was the trouble about the unnatural sort of life they led, as hospital residents. Not only did personal likes and dislikes tend to get out of proportion, but it could be difficult to keep a check on the date, when you spent so much time under one roof.

Tom had told her, when he was last home, that he would telephone her on his arrival in Westhampton. The conference speakers had been booked in at the Royal, which was Westhampton's plushest hotel. So he would ring her in due course if it was today, and meanwhile she had the fracture clinic to attend.

Though she wasn't more than five minutes late it was already in full swing, Mackenzie and Pollock seated at their desks talking to patients, the electric saws whining in the plaster-room and harassed nurses going about their business. Mackenzie might have been expected not to notice one unimportant member of his team, but as Jean slipped into her place behind his desk, where she sat for teaching purposes, he paused for a moment.

'Miss Muir, if I can be on time so can you.'

She muttered an apology, but he had already turned again to the old lady, and was urging her to try and use her shoulder more energetically, if she didn't want it to stiffen up permanently. He could be remarkably patient with frail, deaf old people, an endearing quality, as Jean knew that he wasn't by nature a patient man.

She sat and looked at the back of his dark, well-shaped head, and found it hard to concentrate on the matter in hand, a fact which he soon noticed. Between patients he swivelled his chair round to frown at her.

'Miss Muir, I get the feeling that I'm talking in vain today. Is something on your mind?'

Beneath his bright observant eyes her own fell. 'I'm a bit tired,' she mumbled. 'I—I don't seem able to concentrate.'

He glanced at his watch. 'Coffee in ten minutes, Sister. Miss Muir is in need of refreshment.'

The physiotherapist, the one Jean didn't like, sniggered and made an audible comment to one of the staff nurses that some people had all the luck. The doctors were the only ones who had their coffee brought to them. The nurses and ancillary staff had to make do with hurried breaks when Sister thought it convenient. On a busy morning that might be never.

Jean made a great effort to concentrate. Mackenzie was a first-class teacher, stimulating and thought-provoking. He was in the middle of a brief discourse on Potts' fractures, when a staff nurse spoke to Sister and Sister leaned forward to tell him something.

'Excuse me, sir, there's someone to see Dr Muir.'

'Not now,' he said impatiently. 'Tell whoever it is to come back later.'

'He's already here, sir. Waiting by the door.'

And there was Tom, making signals at his sister from the door of the plaster-room. Embarrassed, Jean jumped to her feet, excused herself awkwardly and went to his side.

'Tom, honestly! Fancy coming here in the middle of a clinic! We're hectically busy. Mackenzie will be livid.'

Tom glanced over her shoulder. 'Is that the tough-looking character at the near desk? He doesn't look livid to me. In fact he's too occupied with his patient to waste time on us.'

Jean drew him back from the doorway, found an empty cubicle in the plaster-room and pulled the curtains shut, so that they were on their own.

'You might have rung. When did you arrive?'

Her brother leant his bony frame against the examination couch, looking irritatingly relaxed. He fished in his pocket for a cigarette.

'You can't smoke here,' Jean snapped at him. 'Honestly, Tom! You've worked in hospitals. You should know the rules.'

'Not for years I haven't,' Tom said with a grin. 'Being a research worker has lots of advantages. Do relax, Jean. No one is indispensable. This clinic won't fold because you stop work for five minutes.'

As if to prove him wrong Mackenzie's voice came from somewhere close at hand. 'Where the devil is Miss Muir?' The curtains swung back, and he looked in, exasperated. 'My dear girl, you cannot wander off in the middle of a clinic, for a chat with your'—he gave Tom an intimidating glare—'friend.'

'Brother, actually,' Tom said disarmingly. 'My apologies for bursting in like this. I did ring, but your switchboard can't have passed on the message.'

Mackenzie's scowl relaxed. 'You must be the chap who's come up for that computer course? Make yourself comfortable somewhere and you can join us for coffee shortly. Sister, put Dr Muir in your office, would you?'

Sister, who regarded her office as her private sanctuary, didn't look too pleased but sent Tom off with a junior nurse, while Jean followed her chief to another cubicle.

'I'm sorry about my brother,' she murmured, and he gave her an amused look.

'So long as it is your brother. I though it was another of your admirers, making a nuisance of himself!'

She coloured and was glad that his attention was already on the patient. When the coffee break came Tom joined them, and with his usual self-assurance made himself very much at home.

'I've got a problem,' he told them. 'Some muck-up over the hotel bookings, so they haven't a room for me. I'm hoping you can put me up in the residents' quarters, Jean.'

'We only have one room for visitors and that's in use. I suppose you could sleep on the common-room sofa?' Jean suggested doubtfully.

'I could, but I don't intend to,' Tom said firmly. 'One of your friends, then? You must know someone who could put me up?'

Liz's parents? She didn't know them very well. The Pollocks? But he had been rather cool lately and she didn't like to ask. Besides, he was sitting right beside them and must have heard the conversation. If he felt like it he would offer.

'I have a spare room,' Mr Mackenzie said.

'Tom couldn't possibly——' Jean began quickly, but her brother cut in with airy acceptance.

'Fine. I'd be most grateful.'

'But, Tom——'

No one listened to her. The men fixed it up and Tom departed to the residents' quarters, shown the way by the prettiest of the staff nurses. Tom always had things going his way, Jean thought, mainly because he made sure that they did. It would never have occurred to him that his sister might be embarrassed if he hobnobbed with her chief.

'Cheer up, little one,' Mackenzie said as he marched her off to see the next patient. 'Your brother will be quite happy with me.' His smile mocked her, not too unkindly, and Jean thought that he must be a mind-reader.

'It's very kind of you,' she began, but he was already intent on examining a child in a frog plaster, and her words fell on deaf ears.

The house surgeons usually stayed in the fracture clinic after their seniors had finished, applying new plasters, or doing any one of a dozen minor surgical procedures. Jean, supporting a child's leg, while Peter slapped on plaster bandages, worried away about Tom.

'He'll be O.K.,' Peter said reassuringly. 'Someone will take him to lunch if we're late.'

He was right. When they looked into the common-room an hour later no one was there, so they went to the dining-room to find Tom sitting at the top table with the senior medical staff. He was carrying on an animated conversation with Mackenzie and one of the pathologists, his thin clever face intent and quite oblivious of his surroundings.

'Only luncheon meat left,' Peter said disgustedly, as they slipped into their places. 'Is that brother of yours as brainy as he looks?'

'More, if anything,' Jean sighed. 'I hope he's not telling Mackenzie how to run his unit.'

Peter gave her an understanding smile. 'You're not too happy about it, are you? Alex putting him up?'

'It makes it awkward,' Jean said uneasily. 'Him of all people!'

'Perhaps it will be the beginning of a lovely friendship,' Peter suggested. 'You can return his hospitality by inviting him to your home!'

'Oh, do shut up, Peter! Actually, he's so busy he'll scarcely see Tom, and Tom will be lecturing all day.'

'You hope,' Peter supplemented.

People were getting up from the other table and drifting towards the door. The pathologist, pausing just behind Jean's chair, told Tom how much he had enjoyed their discussion. Tom raised a hand to him and leant over Jean.

'Alex Mackenzie is taking me out to dinner this evening. Wants you to come too.'

Jean stared at him rather blankly.

'He says you're off duty. About seven, then?'

'I don't know where he lives,' Jean murmured, trying hard to think of a reason for refusing.

'I'll pick you up,' Mackenzie announced.

She swung round in her chair to look at him. 'I'm sure you and Tom would prefer to go on your own. I mean, you don't have to invite me.'

'I'm aware of that, my dear Jean,' he said, with the patient air of one speaking to a retarded child. 'But we should like you to come. I'll meet you in the main hall. Seven sharp.'

'Yes, sir,' Jean muttered rebelliously to his departing back. 'What are you going to do now, Tom?'

'Go over to the post-graduate centre,' said Tom, 'until Alex is free to take me round to his place. Another girl's coming too.'

Pauline, probably. 'How nice,' Jean said with such marked lack of enthusiasm that both Tom and Peter burst out laughing.

'You don't have to come if you hate the idea that much,' said Tom. 'Though he seems a decent type to me. What's the objection?'

She found that a difficult question to answer. A week ago she would have said that she didn't want to go out with a man she disliked so heartily. Now her feelings were more complicated. Last night she had decided that the less she saw of her chief the better—apart, that was, from her duty sessions with him.

'No objection,' she said slowly, and Peter enlarged on the theme.

'We're lowly house surgeons, Dr Muir,' he explained. 'We're not used to hobnobbing with the great.'

'Jean is,' Tom asserted, and Jean coloured slightly.

'At home, Tom. Not here. But don't go on about it, please. I can't back out without looking rude, can I?'

'Seven sharp,' Mackenzie had said, and Jean knew better than to be late. She wore her hair loose on her shoulders, which she never did on duty, and he commented on it when they met.

'You look very sweet, but about sixteen years old. Was that the effect you intended?'

'I didn't intend any effect,' Jean said rather sharply, and he laughed as he unlocked the car for her.

'What liars women are! Of course they try to create an effect, or why do they spend such hours in front of their mirrors?'

'I spent five minutes in front of mine. That was all I had time for.'

'That's obviously my cue to say you don't need embellishing. Fishing for compliments, my dear?'

He was in high good humour and at his most provoking. Jean looked out of the window as the car slid into the main stream of traffic, determined not to rise.

'Where is Tom?' she asked.

'Entertaining our other guest. I've booked a table for eight, so I thought we'd have a drink at my place first.'

'Your other guest?' Jean was deliberately casual. 'Who is she?'

'An old friend of yours,' he said blandly, and when she didn't rise, 'Don't you want to know who?'

'I've already asked, but if you want to make a mystery of it please do.' She was pleased with the cool way she managed that.

'Snubbed,' he murmured, and relapsed into silence.

He lived in an oldish block of flats on the far side of town, well away from the industrial areas. Jean looked at the wide well-kept lawns and immaculate flower-beds.

'Not as nice as your cottage,' she observed, standing by

while he locked up.

'Not to be compared,' he agreed. 'But the terms of my contract state that I have to live within ten miles of the hospital when on duty. It's convenient and it's comfortable.'

In the lift he paused for a moment before pressing the button. 'By the way, Jean, you seem rather prickly tonight. Any reason?'

There were of necessity standing close together in the small lift. Her heart thumped alarmingly in her chest, but she shook her head with a smile. He didn't seem satisfied, however, because he gave a faint frown.

'Relax, my dear girl. We're off duty, remember.'

He unlocked the door of his flat and stood aside for her to enter. Tom's voice sounded from behind a closed door.

'In you go. Don't be shy,' he said, taking her arm as he opened the door of the living-room.

Tom was sprawled in a deep armchair, very much at home, and opposite him, not quite so much at ease, sat Liz Davies.

'Liz!' Jean exclaimed, astonishment mixed with delight, and then indignantly to her chief, 'You might have told me!'

'A pleasant surprise, I gather,' he said softly. 'I wonder who you expected to meet?'

He knew quite well, of course, but Jean didn't mind his teasing, because she was so pleased to see Liz. She joined the other girl on the sofa and accepted a drink. Liz looked more relaxed now, but as always hadn't made the best of herself. The rather ordinary green dress did nothing for her dark brown hair and sallow complexion. Her mind, however, wasn't at all ordinary. She was quick-witted and positive in her views, and in no time was involved in a fierce argument with Tom on the subject of heart transplants.

They seemed to stimulate each other, and Mackenzie for once appeared quite willing to take a back seat. The restaurant he took them to was first class, and Tom confessed that he hadn't expected anything as good in Westhampton.

'A typical arrogant Londoner, aren't you?' the other man asked. His eyes, amused rather than offended, rested on Jean's cocky young brother, and rather surprisingly Tom looked a bit abashed.

'Did I sound arrogant? I didn't mean to.' He glanced at Liz. 'You're a Midlander, aren't you? No offence meant.'

'None taken,' Liz smiled. Well wined and dined, she was happier and more attractive than Jean had ever seen her. Was Mackenzie interested in her after all, and not in Pauline Chalmers? He was the type of man who gave nothing away. He obviously liked Liz, but did it go any further than that? Jean hoped, with a sudden fierce intensity, that it didn't.

'Why so quiet, Jean?'

His long fingers lay for a moment on her bare arm, with electrifying effect. She only prevented herself from jerking her arm back by digging her nails into her palm, but perhaps he felt the tightening of her muscles, because he took his hand away.

Liz and Tom were arguing again with a great deal of good-humoured laughter. 'Feeling left out?' he queried. 'Your friend is getting all the attention, isn't she?'

'He's my brother, Mr Mackenzie,' said Jean. 'He'd hardly show much interest in me.'

'But I'm not your brother,' he answered, leaning slightly towards her and lowering his voice. 'And how about dropping the formality? My name is Alex.'

His dark eyes smiled into hers. Did he guess the effect he had on her? Did it amuse him to disturb her?

'I find it difficult to think of you by your christian name,' she said stiffly, and caught the flicker of irritation on his face before he spoke.

'Awkward little cuss, aren't you? Not prepared to give an inch. I wonder why.'

He turned away from her and said something to the others, leaving Jean unhappily aware that she had behaved very gauchely. She was glad when the time came for them to leave, but dismayed when she understood the arrangements for seeing Liz and her home.

Alex drove them all back to his place and parked beside Tom's car in the forecourt. It appeared to be already agreed that Tom was taking Liz home to her parents, because she was off duty.

'You can drop me at the hospital on your way,' said Jean.

Tom shook his head. 'Too complicated. I don't know my way round the centre of Westhampton. Alex can take you.'

Offhandedly deserted by her brother, who was already helping Liz into his car, Jean could have hit him. 'What a nerve!' she stammered, as he revved up and shot out of the parking lot.

In the half dark she couldn't see the expression on Alex's face, only that he was looking down at her.

'It seems we're stuck with each other,' he said, a hint of laughter in his voice, and added hastily, 'Not that I've any objection.'

Jean got into his car, too preoccupied with Tom's odd behaviour to spare much thought for her own feelings.

'Tom and Liz,' she said slowly, half to herself. 'You don't think ... ?' Her words tailed off.

'I certainly do think.' He sounded rather amused about it, and Jean couldn't resist adding, 'Then you don't mind?'

'Mind? Why the devil should I mind? What funny idea have you got hold of now?' And when she didn't answer he added caustically, 'Dear God, what impossible creatures women are! Sometimes I feel like marrying just to protect myself from this sort of nonsense. I am not, Miss Muir, I repeat not, in the least interested in your friend, greatly as I admire her qualities as a nurse. So if your brother fancies her good luck to him.'

He inserted the key in the ignition but didn't turn it on.

Instead he flicked the lights on inside the car and turned towards her.

'I'm sorry, my dear, it's not you I'm getting at, but the unfortunate tendency of hospital staff to gossip about each other's affairs.'

She said quickly, 'I know exactly what you mean. I've experienced it myself, if you remember.'

She was thinking of Sefton Chalmers and he took her meaning at once.

'So you have,' he agreed drily, and started the engine up.

'Will Tom be moving into the hotel later?' she asked after a minute or two.

'No point, really. He might as well stay on with me. He's only here for four days, isn't he? And by the way, isn't Tom the brother you once compared me with? I don't see much resemblance. I have my fair share of failings, I don't doubt, but I haven't quite such a good opinion of myself!'

Critical of Tom herself, she was quick to jump to his defence when others condemned him. 'He's not really as cocky as he seems. It's just that he's terribly clever—and—and used to getting his own way. I hope he doesn't hurt Liz. She might take him seriously.'

'Let's not start agonising about that now,' he said impatiently. 'They're both adult and in their right minds. You're too fond of interfering in other people's affairs, Jean, though I know you do it with good intentions.'

He turned into the hospital car park, and was out and opening her door before she could do it herself. Anxious to get rid of her, no doubt! From his point of view the evening had probably been a dull one, and would have been more enjoyable if he had invited Pauline instead of her.

'Thank you for the marvellous meal. And for bringing me home.' She brought the words out mechanically, like a well-drilled child, and his eyebrows went up.

'Relieved to be back? Off to bed with you. We're on duty

this weekend, so that means we'll be short of sleep for the next forty-eight hours.'

The weekend turned out to be as busy as Alex Mackenzie had predicted. Jean had thought she might go to one of Tom's lectures, if she left a message with switchboard to say where she was. It proved impossible, however, but Peter, who was off duty, went to the first one.

'What was it like?' Jean asked, and he pulled a horrible face.

'Frightful! Way above my head. It's a very specialised field, of course. And guess who I met there! Liz Davies! And she actually seemed to be enjoying it.'

Perhaps she was more interested in the speaker than the subject, Jean thought. She hadn't seen Tom since Friday evening, but he had telephoned and, in passing, referred to their outing with Alex Mackenzie.

'I like your friend Liz. Splendid girl. Pity I won't be here long enough to get to know her properly.'

'London isn't that far from Westhampton,' Jean pointed out, and he had laughed and said carelessly that she knew the old saying, a bird in the hand. From which Jean took him to mean that though he had taken a fancy to Liz, he wasn't prepared to go to too much trouble to see her again.

Tom had lots of girl-friends, whom he treated very casually. Jean hoped that if he did see Liz again while he was in Westhampton, he wouldn't cause her any heartache.

Liz had no steady boy-friend, didn't get invited out much, and consequently didn't have a great deal of confidence in her own attraction. She could fall quite hard for Tom, Jean thought, wondering if she might ring her friend up and see how the land lay.

Then she remembered Alex's remark that she interfered too much in other people's affairs, and decided to wait until Liz brought the matter up.

On Sunday evening a multiple pile-up on the motorway

meant six hours' hard work in the operating theatre. Peter, who was off duty, but had volunteered his services, helped Pollock in one theatre, while Jean worked with her chief in the other.

When the last patient had been wheeled away to the ward they relaxed for a few minutes in the surgeons' room over coffee and sandwiches. Pollock, inclined to be finicky, always had Horlicks.

'Coffee keeps me awake,' he said morosely.

'Not a bad thing when one's on duty,' Alex remarked.

Pollock gave a grudging smile. 'Maybe, but I'm for bed now, in the hopes that nothing more will come in.'

Jean took this as a hint to depart, so that the men could get changed. She drank her coffee in Sister's office while she wrote up the operation notes. The night nurses were still in Theatre cleaning up, so she was alone when Alex came in a few minutes later.

'I want to look at one or two of those patients before I go home. Are you nearly finished?'

'I can do the notes later if you're in a hurry.'

'No, they're best written while things are fresh in your mind. I'll wait.'

He leant against the wall near the table where she sat, and flicked one of the folders open to read what she had written. She found it difficult to concentrate now, and rubbed her forehead in exasperation as she tried to collect her thoughts.

'Tired?' he asked, his voice gentler than usual. 'I'll do the last one,' and he hooked a chair up to the table and sat down beside her.

Peter's voice sang out from the door. 'I'm off to bed Jean. Pollock and the boss have already gone. Which reminds me, I never enquired how you enjoyed your date with the great man.'

He swung on the door, smiling at Jean, opened it a little wider and saw Mackenzie too. The smile was wiped off his face in a comical fashion.

'I thought you—you'd left, sir,' he stuttered. 'I—uh—I didn't mean to interrupt.'

He withdrew his head quickly and they heard the Theatre doors swinging violently as he departed.

If Jean was put out her chief didn't appear to be. 'It seems I was being unfair to women,' he observed. 'Men gossip too. That lad is a bit cheeky, but I like him. Keen as mustard. Why does he hang around the hospital so much when he's off duty?'

'He hasn't got a proper home,' Jean explained. 'His father is dead and his mother remarried. Peter doesn't get on too well with his stepfather, so his home is wherever his work is.'

'Hmm. Not good for him to get too involved in hospital life, although an extra pair of hands was very useful tonight. Perhaps he hangs around because of you.' He tacked the last remark on so casually that it took her a few seconds to grasp his meaning.

'Of course not! Peter has a girl-friend, one of the radiographers. That pretty one with red hair. Honestly, if you'll forgive me for saying so, you're just as bad as the rest of us, Mr Mackenzie. With less excuse, because you don't spend so much time shut up in here.'

'You make it sound like a prison, my dear girl. Don't you like your work?'

'I love it,' she said earnestly, 'but I shall be glad when I can live out. Being a resident gets me down sometimes.'

'Not really a suitable life for a woman,' he agreed, scribbling the final words on his notes. 'Finished? Good, we'll go and see that mother and daughter first. They were the worst cases.'

The new admissions were all satisfactory. As they left the men's ward the staff nurse on duty, having wished Mr Mackenzie a polite, 'Good night, sir,' asked Jean to write up a sedative for old Mark Thompson.

'He's always inclined to be restless, but tonight he's really climbing the wall. Complaining of pain in the chest too.'

'Better have a look at the old chap,' said Alex. 'I'll wait for you in the office.'

Jean went back into the ward, and behind the curtains that were drawn around Mr Thompson's bed. The bed rails were up to stop him falling out. In the subdued light it was hard to judge his colour. Pain in the chest could spell something serious like a coronary. She checked his pulse and blood pressure and listened carefully to his heart.

'I think you've got a bad go of indigestion,' she told him finally. 'I'll write you up for something that should help.'

'Not surprising after that macaroni cheese,' he said grumpily. 'I told Sister I can't eat cheese at night, but she wouldn't listen to me.'

Jean helped him to button up his pyjama jacket, painfully aware of how frail the old man had become lately. He caught her smooth young hand in his spidery old one, and gripped it tightly.

'You're a lovely girl, Doctor Muir. The nicest of them all. Has he gone now?'

'Has who gone?'

'Mr Mackenzie.' The old man beckoned her closer. 'Sweet on him, aren't you? I've watched you when go round together.'

Jean straightened up, annoyed with herself for blushing. 'Mr Thompson, I don't think——'

'Now I've offended you. I didn't mean to, Doctor. It's just that lying here I see a great deal. I can tell you a lot about the love life of the nurses too. That little pro——'

'No, Mr Thompson!' Jean was torn between indignation and amusement. After all, the old man had little enough entertainment. He wasn't a reader and he couldn't see the television too well from his bed.

He still had her hand in a tight grip. 'If you want him I

hope you get him.' His faded old eyes were more alive than usual. 'Though I'm not sure he's the man for you.'

'Mr Thompson, you must stop it,' and then, weakening, she added, 'Why not?'

'He's a hard man, that one! Likes his own way. Gets it too, doesn't he? His wife's bound to have a tough time.'

'This is a perfectly ridiculous conversation,' Jean said repressively, and pulled her hand out of his. 'And don't you dare talk about it to anyone else!'

He gave her a sly look. 'Now what do you take me for? It's our secret, isn't it?' He was still laughing softly to himself as she left the ward.

'What the devil took you so long?' Alex asked, as she joined him in Sister's office. 'Singing the old man to sleep?'

'He rambles on so,' Jean said vaguely. 'It's difficult to get a proper history from him.' She sank down on to a spare chair to rest her aching legs, tired to the point of confusion. 'Surely there's no one else to see?' she asked wearily.

He looked remarkably fresh for a man who had been operating half the night, his dark eyes alert, his firm mouth quirked a little at the corners in a characteristic half smile. An attractive face, she admitted now, if you found toughness and self-assurance attractive.

'I've told the Night Sisters not to call you again before morning,' he said. 'Short of an emergency that needs all hands, of course.'

'That's very kind of you,' she murmured. 'But if the wards want me?'

'They can contact me.' He glanced at his watch. 'Nearly three. Not worth going back to my flat. I shall manage on the common-room couch for what's left of the night.'

This quite unexpected thoughtfulness for her welfare was not as welcome as it might have been. She didn't want him thinking that girls weren't up to the work, and when she tried, haltingly, to say so, he cut her short abruptly.

'Rubbish, my dear. I'm not trying to get at you, but this

job is too tough for a woman. Sir Geoffrey should never have appointed you.' He looked her up and down critically. 'A big beefy girl like Liz Davies might be able to take it, I suppose, but you haven't the physique for it.'

'I don't think you're being very fair. I work as hard as Peter, but he gets tired too sometimes.'

'We all get tired,' he agreed, 'but the men have to do it if they want to get on in their careers. You don't. At least I take it you've no ambition to be a surgeon?'

'Of course not. But you know I have to do a six-month job in surgery or I wouldn't get on the Medical Register.'

'There are plenty of easier surgical jobs going.'

'This one was easy till you came back,' she retorted, her resentment increased by the fact that she knew in her heart he was right.

His mouth compressed and he took a deep breath as if he was trying hard to control himself. 'Go to bed,' he said shortly, and as she slid the office door back, 'how much longer do you have on my firm?'

'Two months.'

'So little? That's a good thing,' and he turned his back on her to pick up one of the patient's notes.

Jean walked slowly down the corridor, and as she went her eyes filled with tears. So he would be glad when she left, because he regarded her as a nuisance, an inadequate member of his otherwise efficient team. The door of the Night Sisters' office was open, and someone called to her, but Jean went past with averted head and up to her bedroom.

She kicked her shoes off and dropped face downwards on to her bed, her tired mind full of the shattering thought that she had fallen hopelessly, irrevocably in love with a man whom even now she didn't really like. He's not my type, she told herself unhappily, and I'm certainly not his. And if Mr Thompson had noticed the effect he had on her, how many other people might not have done the same? Even more painful than the fact that he was indifferent to her, would be his scorn if he guessed her feelings.

He could, on occasion, be kind, as he had been tonight in offering to stand in for her, an unheard-of thing for a consultant. But he probably only wanted to prove his point that women weren't fit for this sort of work. She rolled over on to her back, thought dejectedly that she must get up and undress properly, but felt too exhausted to make the effort.

The room was always too hot anyway, because the central heating pipes ran round the skirting board. She drifted off into an uneasy sleep, and woke early feeling rumpled and unrefreshed.

## CHAPTER TEN

WHAT she needed more than anything was a bath and a cup of tea. It had just gone seven, so she had time to soak before the other residents started pounding on the door in their haste to be on duty.

She dressed slowly afterwards, feeling a weariness that was more of the mind than the body, and cast a dispirited glance in her mirror. Her pale face and darkly shadowed eyes told their own story. She twisted her hair into a knot on the nape of her neck, because that was the easiest way to wear it in Theatre, and went down to breakfast.

It was an unpleasant shock to find Alex there, though as he had said he wasn't going home, she might have expected it. He sat alone at the residents' table, while a maid put toast and coffee and cereal in front of him.

'Are you sure you don't fancy bacon and eggs, sir?' she asked, and he gave an expressive shudder.

'No, thanks, and from the look of her Dr Muir won't either.'

'No, not for me,' said Jean, and sat down at the far end of the table.

'If I've been up half the night I can't face a large breakfast,' he remarked, and Jean nodded her agreement, fully occupied with the effort needed to maintain her composure.

If life was to be at all bearable for her last months on the Unit, she must summon every ounce of her pride and self-respect, and not give herself away.

'You don't look as if you slept very well,' he continued, eyeing her narrowly.

'There wasn't much left of the night, was there? I hope you weren't disturbed again.'

'Only once.' The maid had returned with a fresh supply

of toast and coffee and he beckoned to her. 'Put it over here, please. Miss Muir is moving.' And to Jean he added, 'I feel like those people in the TV advert, shouting at each other down the ancestral table. Move over, for heaven's sake!'

She moved reluctantly, picking up a newspaper on the way, so that she would have some defence against him. She propped it up in front of her coffee pot, murmured, 'You don't mind?' and read it steadily, without taking in much of the meaning.

After a few minutes she looked up and met his eyes, faintly quizzical and also puzzled. 'I have the impression I'm getting the brush-off,' he said.

'What an extraordinary thing to say.' She was proud of the careless way she produced that. 'I mean, how could an H.S.——'

'Spare me a dissertation on our relative status, which seems to obsess you, for some reason.' He looked thoroughly exasperated now. 'You're cross about something, little Miss Muir, and I'm damned if I know why. I should have thought that even I might have rated a little friendliness for trying to spare you last night.'

She bit her lip, feeling rather ashamed of herself. 'Of course I'm grateful,' she said, lowering her voice because another young doctor had just come in. 'But it would have been nicer if you hadn't been so patronising about it. And—and no one likes to be told they're not wanted.'

Now what on earth had made her say that? She lowered her eyes again to her newspaper, thankful that the house physician had sat herself down close enough to make discretion necessary.

Mackenzie's voice was abrasive now. 'We'll continue this conversation in my office, Miss Muir. In five minutes, please.'

'The list——' she murmured.

'It's only eight-thirty. Allow me to pour you a cup of this

singularly unattractive coffee.' His expression was as disagreeable as his voice. 'Five minutes,' he repeated, and pushed back his chair abruptly.

'What was all that about?' the house physician asked, wide-eyed.

'Oh, mind your own business!' Jean snapped, with quite uncharacteristic rudeness, and then, because she liked the other girl, she apologised.

'I've heard he's very trying to work for,' the house physician said sympathetically. 'I take it he's about to tear a strip off you?'

'I suppose so,' Jean agreed glumly, and tried to sort out her thoughts so that she could put up a sensible defence. Best really to say that her emotional outburst had been due to tiredness, even if that confirmed his opinion that women were very much the weaker sex.

They met outside his door just as he was locking it. 'Sefton insists on seeing me before the list starts,' he said tersely. 'You can come along with me and explain that extraordinary remark on the way.'

'Oh, please, it was just silly——'

'Come on.' He took her arm in a hard grip and marched her off, down the long main corridor. 'Well, Miss Muir? I'm waiting.'

'It was silly of me...' Her voice faltered.

'Very silly, but what did it mean? That childish remark about being unloved and unwanted?'

'I didn't put it quite like that,' she said despairingly, near to tears. 'If you'd stop a moment.' She was panting with the effort of keeping up with him, but he walked her on regardless, to the lift that took them up to the private wing.

He pressed the 'Call' button and turned to her. 'Well?'

'You said you would be pleased when I finished,' she said, low-voiced, 'and it may be true, but I think it was—was—rather unkind to tell me.'

The lift whirred down. He crashed the door open,

bundled her in and crashed it shut again. He stood quite still, one hand near the button, the other still on her arm.

'I knew a woman on the firm meant trouble,' he said wearily. 'Even the cleverest girl seems to take everything so personally. Do you think if I'd made the same remark to young Davidson he'd have reacted like this?'

'He might not have shown it, but I don't suppose he'd have liked it. I've tried hard to be an adequate H.S.'

He drew in his breath sharply and to her mortification began to laugh. 'You're more than adequate, you little fool. Davidson and you are the best couple I've had since I've been here. And just for the record, I thought it was a good thing you were finishing soon, because you look as if you need a holiday.'

The lift stopped at the fourth floor. 'Satisfied?' he asked, and she nodded, feeling a complete fool.

'I'm—sorry. I expect I misunderstood because I was tired.'

'I expect you did.'

'I'll see you in Theatre, then.'

'No, you're coming with me. To see our mutual friend,' and when she hung back, 'For God's sake, girl, don't be tiresome all the time!'

So she trailed after him reluctantly and stood just inside the door of Mr Chalmers' room with a carefully composed face, while her chief and his most troublesome patient exchanged a few sharp words.

'I said you could go home next week if the X-rays were all right. They're not, so discharge is out of the question.'

'I can lie in bed at home. What's wrong with a private nurse?' Sefton grunted. 'You've said yourself I'm through the worst.'

'I can't trust you not to overdo it. And you'd probably drink too much, which wouldn't do that damaged liver any good.'

Sefton's face became suffused with colour. 'I'm not a

complete fool, Alex. But I could run my business affairs better from home.'

'No.'

'And if I simply discharge myself?'

'Then you can find yourself another surgeon,' Alex rasped. 'I'm not having all that hard work I put in on you wasted.'

'Charming,' sneered Sefton. 'So it's the waste of time that would upset you, not what might happen to me?'

'You'd have brought it on yourself, wouldn't you?'

'Oh, stop it!' Jean cried, and they both turned astonished faces towards her. Beyond a flicker of a smile in her direction when they first came in, Sefton had paid her no attention, because he had launched straight into his attack on Alex.

'You keep out of this, Miss Muir,' Alex snapped, but she shook her head.

'I won't! You ought to be ashamed of yourself, Mr Chalmers, for being so unreasonable. You're lucky to be alive, and the least you can do is to co-operate.'

Alex smiled broadly. 'I couldn't have put it better myself. Perhaps you'll pay more attention to Jean than to me, eh?'

The older man lay back against his pillows, his bottom lip stuck out like a sulky child's. 'All right, all right,' he said ungraciously to Jean. 'So you've gone over to the enemy, my dear?'

'That's a funny way to talk about your surgeon,' Jean said with a determined effort at lightness.

'But not unjustified, damn it. He may have done a good job on me, but does it give him the right to lay down the law? And what about the way he interfered between you and me? Preferring to listen to that idiot daughter of mine?' He was working himself up into an alarming passion, and Mackenzie wasn't helping by showing open amusement.

Jean trod on his foot hard, and he swore under his breath, and stopped smiling.

'Mr Chalmers, please don't excite yourself,' she said gently, 'I know Mr Mackenzie's rather tactless——'

'Look here, Miss Muir——'

'But he's the same to us all. Please do what he says.' She laid her hand on his and gave him a pleading look.

'I've said I would,' Sefton said a trifle gruffly, 'but I can't wait to get out. And when I do'—he laid his other hand on top of hers—'I hope you'll come and visit me at home.'

'I shall be delighted to,' Jean promised, a touch of defiance in her manner as she looked at her chief.

He eyed them sardonically. 'Touching. And now that you've sorted out my problems for me, Miss Muir, shall we be on our way?'

'I hope you'll forgive me for interfering,' Jean said a trifle breathlessly, as he shut Sefton's door behind them with a decided bang.

He stalked along to the lift before he answered her, and when she caught up with him she saw that his face was a mass of conflicting emotions. Exasperation, amusement, anger came and went. 'Do you know where I'd like to be right now, my dear girl? At the cottage alone with you, with no one around to prevent me teaching you a lesson.'

Jean's chest felt curiously tight. 'I did say I was sorry,' she whispered.

'And so you darned well ought to be! You have a nerve, interfering with my private patients! And what the devil did you mean telling that old rogue that I'm tactless?'

'You weren't exactly handling him with kid gloves.'

'He doesn't deserve it.'

'He's been very ill.'

'That doesn't excuse him. He gives the nurses one hell of a time too.'

'Then why not let him go home? They're so rich they

could afford a day and a night nurse, couldn't they? And a physiotherapist—the lot, in other words.' She stopped quickly when she saw that his expression had changed to one of controlled anger.

'Keep out of it. It has nothing to do with you. And don't look at me like that——' his voice was harsh now. 'Girls who play on their feminine charm are apt to get more than they bargain for.'

The lift had arrived and she walked into it and stood with her back to him. 'I don't put on an act,' she said, low-voiced, directing her remark at the wall before her. 'I can't help it if I'm—I'm reasonably attractive. I know you'd like me better if I was plain.'

He had come to stand just behind her. She dug her hands into the pockets of her white coat and thought, unhappily, that it was no good, however hard she tried. There was something about their personalities that led to scenes like this.

The same thought must have been in his mind, because as the lift reached the ground floor he spoke. 'I shouldn't necessarily like you better, Miss Muir, I should just find you easier to handle.'

He made no move to open the doors and she turned round slowly, to catch a strange expression on his face. 'I've had about as much as I can take——' his hand hovered for a moment near her cheek, then he withdrew it sharply and jerked the lift door back. 'If this goes on much longer I shall need a holiday too,' he said savagely, and walked out of the lift without waiting for her.

Jean's legs felt as though they were going to give way under her, so she leant against the wall for a few moments. In a muddled sort of way she understood what Alex had meant. He had practically acknowledged the strength of the attraction between them. Unfortunately it didn't make him like her more. Rather, he had implied, the reverse.

*

Tom telephoned that evening to say that he wouldn't be seeing her again before he left. 'I'm taking Liz out to dinner. You don't mind, do you?'

'Mind? I'm delighted. Oh, you mean because you're not taking me too. Idiot! I don't fancy playing gooseberry.'

She spoke to Liz next morning to find out if the other girl was free that afternoon. 'It's my half day and it's a lovely one. We could go out in the country.'

Liz was not too keen. 'I'm on duty tonight, and I thought I'd have a nap this afternoon.'

'But you've been off for lots of nights,' Jean persisted, unsuccessfully, however. Liz just didn't want to go out.

It seemed she didn't want to talk about Tom either. That evening, coming in after a hot and unenjoyable solo drive, Jean called in at the Night Sisters' office for a cup of tea. Liz gave her a rather wan smile and concentrated on hospital business, taking less part than usual in the good-humoured banter the younger residents indulged in.

Jean sat on until the room cleared, but Liz, briskly efficient in her immaculate navy uniform, went into the Night Superintendent's office, and clearly didn't intend coming out for some time. Her face had a strained look and Jean thought ruefully that her parting from Tom had not been a happy one.

She was off next weekend and had decided to go home, but on the Friday evening Tom telephoned quite late, and she took the call in the office. 'Jean? I've decided to come up this weekend. Mother says you're due here tomorrow, so I can have your bedroom, can't I?'

Astonishment kept her quiet for a moment. 'No objection, I take it?' he asked sharply.

'No, I suppose not, but Tom——'

The telephone was on Liz's desk, and when she heard Tom's name she became very still.

'Why are you coming?' Jean asked, and he made a curious sound.

'Because I want to see Liz, of course.'

'Hang on.' Jean put her hand on the mouthpiece and bent towards her friend. 'Liz,' she said urgently, 'Tom wants to come up this weekend—to see you. Are you free?'

Liz went fiery red and then pale. 'I'm on nights till Monday. It's no good.'

'But you're free by day. You can sleep any time,' Jean said impatiently, restraining an urge to shake her. An angry babble came from the telephone. 'Oh, Tom, do be quiet! Just hang on a moment,' and to Liz she said in exasperation, 'Don't you want to see him?'

'Of course,' Liz muttered, eyes downcast, 'but why couldn't he ring me?'

'He wanted to ask if my room would be free. He was probably going to ring you afterwards.' She spoke into the telephone again. 'Yes, Tom, I'll fix it up. And, Tom, I'm in the office. Liz is right here if you want to speak to her.'

'Why didn't you say so?' Tom asked crossly. 'Put me on to her, then,' and Jean handed over the phone to a miraculously transformed Liz.

The only person who had been a close and interested observer of this little scene was Peter Davidson. He pulled one of his comical faces at Jean and jerked his head at the door. 'Come on,' he murmured. 'Leave them to it.' Outside he gave a horrible leer. 'Is something going between those two? How odd. I'd never have thought they'd have a thing in common.'

'Don't joke about it, Peter. Liz is serious at any rate. Too serious, I'm afraid.'

'Well, so must he be,' Peter pointed out, 'or he wouldn't be coming back so soon.' He became unusually thoughtful. 'Psychology has always interested me. You know, what makes some people click just like that. After all, they've only seen each other a few times. And for that matter, what makes some people take an equally instant dislike to each other.'

Like Alex and me, Jean thought sadly. Only in their case perhaps antagonism had been a defence mechanism against a heady attraction. She had managed to keep out of his way all week, beyond a few essential exchanges over work, and those had been made in the company of their colleagues. He was chillingly polite to her on these occasions, and she in return kept a carefully controlled face and voice in his presence. After one punctilious exchange on their last ward round she caught Peter, who was a sharp-eyed lad, giving her a rather speculative look.

On Saturday morning she woke to the telephone's ringing and even as she hooked it off the cradle, thought what a relief it would be to get away from the hospital for two days.

'Jean?' Liz croaked, her voice quite unlike her usual clear tones. 'Please don't go home this weekend. Please stay. I can't face your brother on my own.'

'But, Liz, what is this?'

'I feel at such a disadvantage,' Liz sighed. 'He's only playing about, I know, and I'—her voice cracked for a moment—'I know it's daft when I've only just met him, but I'm crazy about him.'

'Oh, Liz!' Jean thought for a moment. 'But what good will my staying do?'

'Sort of keep things from getting too serious,' Liz mumbled.

'But, Liz, honestly! You're not suggesting I go out with you? Where is Tom meeting you?'

'Here. At the hospital. You haven't planned anything special this weekend, have you? Well then—if you won't stay I shall ring Tom right now and put him off.'

It was quite ridiculous, but there was no doubt that she meant it. So Jean telephoned and told her mother that she wouldn't be coming home after all.

'What a pity,' said Mrs Muir. 'Lise has been cooking all your favourite things.'

'Oh, Mother! I really wanted to come. I've had my fill of hospital this week. But—but my car's out of action——' She lied foolishly on the spur of the moment, thinking the real explanation too complicated.

'Then come by train, silly child,' her mother said crisply.

'The trains are so poor.'

'Haven't you heard of inter-city?' Mrs Muir asked drily, and Jean muttered an unconvincing reply. 'You don't have to make excuses, my dear. If you've something better to do say so. I do dislike people who tell lies. It makes life so difficult.' The telephone clicked as her mother hung up and Jean thought disconsolately that it was hardly a good beginning to the weekend.

Liz had arranged to meet Tom in the hospital forecourt. When he drove in just after eleven he looked surprised to see Jean there as well.

'Didn't Mother tell you I was staying here after all?'

'Yes. She seemed a bit put out,' Tom said absently. He had eyes only for Liz, who looked smarter than usual in a burnt orange skirt and jacket, chosen by Jean, that flattered her friend's rather gipsyish dark colouring.

'Shall we go, then?' he asked, opening the car door for Liz.

Liz cast an anxious look at Jean, who had never felt more foolish in her life. 'You won't mind if I come too, Tom? I'm at a loose end today.'

Tom would probably have made a rude and brotherly reply if Liz hadn't been sitting there. As it was he shut the car door rather hard, gave Jean a furious and incredulous look, and left her to get in or not, as she pleased. She would much rather have stayed, but mindful of Liz's mute appeal, she joined them reluctantly.

No one said anything for a minute or two, and then Tom, his eyes on the busy road, said coolly, 'So if you're staying where do I sleep?'

'The guest-room is free this weekend,' Jean said placatingly. 'Tom, I don't want to put you out——'

'No, no!' Liz rushed in, 'Tom wants you to come, don't you? We wouldn't think of leaving you behind.'

Tom gave a noncommittal grunt, which Jean had no difficulty in interpreting.

'Where are we going?' Liz asked a little too brightly, and he answered briefly, 'For a picnic.' For Jean's benefit he added, 'I've brought some of the food Lise cooked for you.'

Conversation continued in a rather strained and desultory manner, while Jean pondered on the extraordinary way quite sensible well-balanced people could behave when they fell in love. Would Liz insist on her accompanying them again tomorrow, or would her brother, who was accustomed to getting his own way, put his foot down?

She gazed out of the window at a vaguely familiar scene, caught sight of a signpost, and observed, 'Why, we're not far from Mr Mackenzie's cottage. Just a few miles, in fact.'

She felt a bitter-sweet pang as she remembered how she had enjoyed that day, before life had become complicated by tangled emotions.

'That's right,' Tom agreed, and relapsed into silence.

'How do you know?' Jean asked in vague surprise.

'Because he gave me directions, of course. It should be just about three miles from here.'

'You can't mean'—Jean was so agitated that she could hardly get the words out—'we're not going to his place?'

'That's right. I rang him last night and asked him to recommend somewhere pleasant to take Liz. He said why not come here. Jolly decent of him, don't you think?'

'You mean he'll be out himself?' Jean asked hopefully, but her brother turned briefly in his seat to give her a smile of pure malice.

'Oh no. I didn't get that impression. So you can pair off with your boss while I take Liz for a hike. He says there's marvellous country around here.'

Jean looked out at a great shoulder of the Shropshire

hills, and wondered what she had done to deserve a situation like this. Tom didn't want her and Alex certainly wouldn't. Wild ideas of ordering Tom to stop and getting out in the middle of nowhere ran through her mind, but she had left it too late. They swept round a corner, started to climb, and there was the cottage, and Alex doing something to the fence near the white gate.

He turned as the car approached, waved cheerfully and looked surprised when he saw Jean. Tom parked on the grass verge outside. Liz got out quickly and started to say something to Alex about hoping they weren't being a nuisance.

Tom gave his sister a painful nip on the arm as she got out more slowly. 'It's you who're the nuisance,' he muttered in her ear.

'If you'd told me you were coming here——'

'Don't fancy an afternoon with Alex?' he jeered. 'Well, it's poetic justice for being so tactless, my little sister.'

As furious as he was, she hissed back at him, 'Liz begged me to come. She didn't care to be alone with you. And you can make what you like of that!'

She was pleased to see Tom looking shaken, but wondered uneasily if she'd let her friend down.

Alex, having assured Liz that they were no trouble, gave Jean a less warm smile. 'Come up to the cottage and have a drink,' he suggested.

They sat around on the stone-flagged area outside the living-room windows. The two men talked and the girls were both rather quiet. Jean, who had been avoiding her chief's eyes, started when he put a direct question to her.

'You like gardening, don't you? You can stay and help me while the others go off for their picnic.'

She looked at him reluctantly, saw with a sinking heart that his mouth had a nasty twist to it, but didn't feel up to making any resistance.

Tom downed his drink with indecent haste and hustled

Liz off to his car, with detailed instructions from Alex as to where to go. Jean sat on the improvised stone seat and rested her back against the rough wall of the house. The midday sun beat down on her and was reflected off the flagstones. She shut her eyes and waited for the unpleasant moment when Alex would come back.

A bird chirped in the pear tree close at hand. Footsteps crunched on the loose chips of the drive. She kept her eyes shut until he spoke.

'What the devil are you playing at?'

She blinked up at him, dazzled by the sun's glare. 'Don't start anything, please,' she said tiredly. 'I had no idea we were coming here. It was Tom's way of getting his own back, I suppose. I mean, he only told me at the last moment or I wouldn't have come.'

'Getting his own back for what?'

'For—for my tagging along when he wanted Liz to himself.'

'Yes indeed. Not very tactful of you, was it?' he said disagreeably. 'Surely you could have found something else to do?'

'Liz wanted me to come. It's crazy, I know, but she's unsure of herself and—and unsure of Tom. She has an odd idea that there's safety in numbers.' She laughed a little shakily. 'I quite expected her to say it was too hot for walking.'

'Which it is.' His voice was less disagreeable now. 'But I don't think that brother of yours intends to do much walking.'

She shut her eyes again because she felt at a disadvantage with him towering over her.

'Young Tom takes a lot for granted,' he added, 'Dumping you here in this casual fashion.'

She looked up at him quickly, pink with embarrassment. 'You don't have to rub it in. It's not my idea of a pleasant Saturday either. In fact it looks like being a rotten weekend, with Mother annoyed, Tom furious and you making snide remarks.'

She dug her teeth in her bottom lip to stop it trembling, jumped to her feet and felt a curious roaring in her ears. She swayed and would have fallen if he hadn't gripped her hard by both arms.

'Hey! Steady on.' His voice seemed to come from a long way away, then as her vision cleared, she saw concern and an unusually kindly expression on his face. 'Comes of jumping up so suddenly after sitting in the sun. Postural hypotension. Though I'd have thought you poured out enough adrenalin with that impassioned speech to put your blood pressure up again.' He smiled at her and she responded weakly.

'Come into the house where it's cooler,' he said. 'You'll feel better after some lunch.'

He sat her down in a comfortable old armchair, in a corner of the kitchen, while he laid the table.

'Can't I help?'

'Stay where you are. It's only cold stuff. The ham was cooked by my sister. None of your pre-packaged meat for her.'

'Does she enjoy cooking?'

'Yes. And bakes superbly, like most Scotswomen.'

'Don't you regret leaving Scotland?'

'Not really. After my mother's death I was mad keen to get right away—too many unhappy associations. I looked for a job in the Midlands because my sister was already here.'

The food was delicious—thick slices of ham, crisp salad and crusty bread, a large bowl of raspberries with cream.

'I feel better,' Jean said at last, leaning back in her chair and giving him a happy smile.

'You look it. Out there you had me worried for a moment.'

'I did feel awful,' she admitted. 'Why don't you let me wash up and then I'll go for a stroll somewhere.'

'You'll do nothing of the sort. I'm going to put a deck-chair in the shade and you can spend the afternoon lazing in it. And later when it's cooler, you can do some weeding if you really want to.'

'Orders?' she asked cheekily, and he smiled down at her.

'Orders,' he said firmly, so she did as she was told.

It was surprisingly pleasant to sit under the pear tree, in the little orchard to one side of the house. Jean read a not very exciting travel book, picked at random from a selection in the cottage, but spent more time looking around her at the peaceful country scene. She watched Alex too, as he scythed the long grass in the orchard, like one who had been doing it all his life. Quite a change from his boyhood in a grim industrial area, she thought. No wonder he loved it here.

After that initial unpleasant scene he had been remarkably kind, and though he couldn't want her around, he showed no sign of resenting her presence. She resolved not to intrude on him in any way, and hoped that Tom and Liz would come back in good time.

In fact they stayed away until the last possible moment. Jean was on her knees, weeding a small flower-bed, when Tom's car drew up by the gate, and they came swinging up the drive, arm in arm.

Liz's face was blazingly happy, her nose shiny and her clothes rumpled. She looked like a girl who was madly in love and didn't mind showing it. Even Tom, her cool detached rational brother, looked more human than usual.

'We're later than we meant to be,' Tom said. 'Have to make a dash for it or Liz won't be back in time. Are you ready, Jean?' He sounded more friendly now, as well he might be, the afternoon having gone as he had planned.

Jean jumped up, but Alex, striding up to join them, put a hand on her arm. 'I'll bring Jean back later. She doesn't want to go back yet. Do you?' His fingers dug into her soft upper arm.

She took his meaning, yet hesitated because he couldn't really want her to stay. 'It's such a long way for you——'

'Nonsense. Besides, I could do with your help. Please stay.' He smiled down at her very convincingly, and Jean felt a pang of regret that he was only doing this for the others.

'All right.' She managed a bright smile in return, kept it fixed to her face until Tom had roared off down the drive, and then gave him a worried look.

'We're being an absolute drag I'm afraid, Tom and I.'

They were standing by the gate. He didn't bother to reply but said with a frown, 'Twenty is enough on these lanes. I hope your brother doesn't have an accident.'

'Tom's an excellent driver.'

'His mind isn't on the road, though,' he said sardonically. 'What it is to be in love!'

'Do you think they'll get married?'

'Probably.' There was a touch of impatience in his voice now. 'But it's early days and they'll let people know when they want to,' which she took as a warning to drop the subject.

So she went back to her weeding and worked diligently until she had completed the whole bed. The two little boys from down the lane turned up when they were relaxing in the evening sunshine, Alex with a beer and Jean with a cider, ice cold from the refrigerator. They exchanged enthusiastic greetings with Jean and told her about a badger they had seen yesterday by the stream. They were unaffectedly pleased to see her and made it very plain.

Simon, the older boy, asked Alex why she hadn't been back before this.

'She's been busy.'

'Oh. But you did want her to?'

Jean felt a complete fool, but Alex handled it easily. 'She works with me all week, so she wouldn't want to spend her weekends with me too, now would she?'

'If she likes you she would.' That was the little one.

'Ah, but she doesn't.' He gave her a mocking smile.

'Then why——'

'No more questions. Off you go, chaps. I'm just about to make supper.'

'Can we have some?'

'No.' He sounded quite definite about that, had a sip or two of beer and changed his mind. 'Yes, O.K., if you go and tell your mother.'

They rushed off, yelling with excitement, and Jean was conscious of acute disappointment. This would almost certainly be the last time she came to the cottage and she could have treasured the memory of a day that had turned out better than she had expected. A day spent, moreover, mainly alone with Alex.

She gave a little sigh, which unfortunately he heard. 'What's wrong? You don't mind the boys coming. I thought you liked them, unlike Pauline.'

'I do,' she said quickly, and couldn't resist adding, 'Does she come here often?'

'Not often. She has no feeling for the country. Pauline prefers the bright lights.'

They went into the house to start the supper, which Jean insisted on helping with, so he put her on to cutting up a huge mound of chips.

'Egg and chips is their favourite meal. Followed by ice-cream. Bacon and eggs all right for you?'

It turned out to be a happy meal. Jean, accepting disappointment gracefully, laughed and joked with the others. At nine o'clock Alex packed them off, walking down the lane with them while she washed up.

The large old-fashioned kitchen range was burning and he drew up two chairs for them. 'Not worth lighting the fire in the other room. What time do you want to get back?'

'Any time. When it suits you.'

'Why can't you always be so accommodating?' he teased.

'You haven't argued with me for hours.'

'You've been nicer too.' She smiled at him and he met her eyes steadily until she looked away. She was breathing faster than usual and hoped that he didn't notice. She had to occupy herself somehow, so she snatched up the poker and stirred the fire quite unnecessarily.

'Perhaps we had better be on our way to Westhampton now,' he said quietly.

She fiddled with the poker, unhappily aware that he had just changed his mind. Two minutes before he had shown every sign of wanting to relax by the fire. Then why? Because he had guessed at the true state of her feelings?

'Isn't there a station anywhere near?' she asked awkwardly. 'Then you wouldn't have such a long way to go.'

'We're about halfway between Shrewsbury and Ludlow, and I doubt if either has a train to Westhampton at this hour. You could stay the night, of course, and go back some time tomorrow?'

'No,' she said too quickly, and caught the flash of anger on his face before he shrugged and turned away.

'You have the wrong idea, Miss Muir,' he said coldly. 'I do have a spare bedroom.'

Her cheeks burned. She spoke haltingly. 'Well, of course. I know you have. It's kind of you to offer—I didn't think——'

He swung round again and gave her the mocking smile she hated. 'Oh, but you did! It showed on your face. And just for the record, let's get one thing straight. I never get involved with the women I work with. I learnt that lesson years ago. Makes life too complicated.'

Humiliated and unhappy, she followed him to the car. The return journey was a silent one. Jean shut her eyes and pretended to sleep, while brooding over the problem of how to convince Alex that he had been mistaken about her. That she wasn't a silly girl who had fallen in love with him, and who would make his life tiresome and embarrassing.

Just for a moment she thought how wonderful it would have been if she could have taken him up on his offer and stayed the night. To wake in the morning with the happy certainty of another day in his company. How lucky Liz was to be spending tomorrow with the man of her choice!

Her eyes pricked and she felt unpleasantly choked. Cautiously she tried to clear her throat, and he spoke sharply.

'So you're not asleep. Nearly there now.'

Jean sat up and risked a quick blow of her nose. 'I'm sorry I've made you angry again,' she said, her voice coming out a little muffled.

They had stopped at some traffic lights and Alex turned to look at her. 'For God's sake don't cry. I'm the one who should apologise, I suppose. It was inevitable you should assume that I was making a pass at you. Things being the way they are,' he added savagely.

'What do you mean?' she managed, and he snapped back at her.

'You know quite well what I mean. You're well aware of your own charms. And you also know that I'm strongly attracted to you, so don't pretend otherwise. For that matter, I'm darned sure the attraction is mutual.'

'And if it is,' she stammered, 'it's only physical attraction. Which means nothing. Nothing at all, without—without—liking.' Loving was what she really meant, but she couldn't bring herself to say it.

The lights changed and the car took off fast. 'I'm glad you understand that,' he said, his voice controlled again. 'Perhaps you're growing up at last.'

As the car swung through the hospital gates Jean started to unbuckle her safety belt. 'Thank you for bringing me,' she said, her voice bright and impersonal. 'The first part of the day was nice anyway.'

She fumbled at the door, unfamiliar with the handle, and he came round to open it for her. He held her elbow for a moment as he helped her out.

'Can't wait to get away from me, eh? Well, perhaps a little plain speaking has cleared the air. Don't you agree?'

She looked back at him helplessly, trying to think of a reply, and then by a lucky chance she saw Tony, getting out of his car.

'Hey, Tony,' she called. 'Wait a second!' She waved and Tony came across to them, staring when he realised they were together.

'I thought you were on duty,' Alex said sharply, the consultant once again, and Tony smiled and shook his head.

'No, sir. I've swapped weekends.'

'Indeed? I don't remember your asking.'

'I arranged it with Pollock. He didn't mind.'

'It isn't really a question of Pollock minding,' Alex said coldly. 'I like to be informed of what my staff are up to.'

'Well, I think it's splendid,' said Jean, jumping in to divert her chief's attention. 'Now we can drive down to London together. I'm always unhappy on the motorway. Good night, Mr Mackenzie, and thanks a lot for the lift.'

She was aware of his raised eyebrows, and the look of annoyance on his face as she turned away with Tony. 'I don't care,' she thought bitterly, 'if only he'll believe that it's really Tony I'm interested in,' and she thrust her arm through Tony's and launched into an animated conversation.

Tony, a little bemused, asked her please to enlighten him. What was she up to after giving him the cold shoulder for the last few weeks?

'I'm not up to anything,' she assured him, but as they passed through the hospital entrance she couldn't resist a quick backward glance.

She was just in time to see Alex's car reversing at speed out of the car park, and felt more like weeping than carrying on with an act that was no longer necessary.

'Good night, Tony,' she said flatly, and walked off, leaving him staring after her.

## CHAPTER ELEVEN

At breakfast next morning Tony wanted to know if Jean had had too much to drink the previous night.

'Certainly not,' she said crossly. 'What gave you that idea?'

'Your odd behaviour.' He looked only half convinced and Tom, who was sitting with them, said with a grin, 'If she did it was to give herself Dutch courage. She had to spend yesterday with her boss.'

'Had to?'

'We were all at his cottage and Liz and I went off, so that left Jean on his hands.'

'Delightfully put,' Jean muttered, and Tony laughed.

'I'm sure he enjoyed it,' he said kindly. 'I've always thought he has a soft spot for you.'

'What absolute rubbish!'

'Is it? He glares every time he sees us together.'

'You know why,' Jean said under her breath, and Tom turned the conversation before Tony could reply, by jumping to his feet.

'Time to meet Liz. I take it you're not coming with us again?' He gave Jean a brotherly bang on the shoulder and walked out whistling cheerfully, without waiting for her answer.

'At a loose end?' Tony asked. 'Come out with me, then? How about hiring a boat and going on the river? Near that pub I took you to. Remember?'

It sounded a pleasant way of getting through the day. During the long hours on the river Tony told her a good deal about his affairs. He had been in London yesterday, seeing his solicitor, and his divorce would shortly be through.

'Divorce?' Jean asked, startled, and he shrugged.

'Didn't I tell you? I thought I did.'

'You told me you'd parted from your wife, but I didn't realise it was so final. Oh, Tony. You did say you loved her.'

Tony stared. 'Did? How odd!'

Jean was shocked by his casual manner. 'You said the only girl you'd ever loved had given you the push—or something like that.'

His face changed subtly. 'I wasn't talking about my wife. I married her on the rebound. I suppose it was doomed to failure from the start.'

'Oh, Tony!' Disapproval warred with sympathy in Jean's kind heart. 'What a mess. The other girl—is she still free?'

'No!' Tony bit the word out. 'Look, Jean, I don't want to talk about it, O.K.?'

He took her back to the pub for dinner, and on the return journey he parked the car in a lay-by, and this time Jean made no demur. Being kissed by Tony was quite an experience, calculated to drive thoughts of another man out of a girl's mind, at least for the present. She responded to him with a touch of wildness, so that Tony, drawing away from her at last, stared down at her with surprise.

'Well, well,' he said softly, 'you have come on lately.' He reached for her again, but Jean, a little alarmed by her own reaction, pushed him away.

'No, Tony. Let's go back.'

He let her go reluctantly. 'O.K., O.K., I can wait.'

Back at the hospital, Tony suggested calling in at the Office. Jean, who had done nothing more than run a comb through her hair, said, 'I must look a mess.'

Tony gave her a smiling comprehensive glance. 'Actually you look fabulous. Sort of glittery and different. Come on.'

'What nonsense you talk, but you're good for a girl's morale.'

They walked into the office together, still smiling, and there was Alex, on his own with a cup of tea in his hand. Through the door to the inner office Jean could see two of the Night Sisters, busily writing, but none of the junior doctors were around at present.

He gave them a cool good evening and went on with his tea. Tony poured a cup for Jean and himself.

'We've been on the river. That place where we met you once,' he said.

Alex nodded, and watched Jean, whose hand trembled slightly, so that the tea slopped into the saucer.

'Dear me, you are in a state!' The words were innocuous, but his manner wasn't. He took the cup from her and placed it on the desk. 'Sit down, Miss Muir.. Boating must be more—exciting than I realised.' His eyes, hard and unkind, raked her face, making her aware that she probably did look dishevelled after Tony's lovemaking. She pushed nervously at her hair.

'I wish you wouldn't stare at me like that. I didn't have a chance to tidy up.'

'If I was staring,' he mocked her softly, 'it was in admiration.' He eyed her mouth and she put a hand to it with a curious little defensive gesture. He laughed then, rather contemptuously, and turned away to look at some notes on the office desk.

Tony, who had been engaged in filling up the kettle again, missed this little exchange. 'Why are you in, sir?' he asked. 'Trouble?'

'Just wanted to look at some notes. One of the patients on tomorrow's list.'

The discussion became technical and Jean, forgotten, drank her tea quickly and departed. A heavy weight of depression hung over her. She told herself to snap out of it. Hadn't she succeeded admirably in her act with Tony? If only, she thought miserably, Alex hadn't looked at her with such contempt.

To cheer herself up a little she vowed to tell him about Tony's divorce on the first possible occasion. If he knew that she wasn't a girl who broke up marriages, he might not like her any better, but at least he wouldn't despise her.

The opportunity to raise such an awkward subject never seemed to present itself. There weren't many occasions on which a house surgeon was alone with a consultant. Besides, it wasn't the sort of thing one could just launch into without any warning. Most of the time Alex treated her as if she wasn't there. He was equally cool towards Tony, and that young man told her with feeling of an abrasive interview he had had with their chief.

'I asked him if it was O.K. Pollock and I doing a permanent swap. He said no, it wasn't. He didn't want you and me on together at weekends. When I asked him why he gave me one of his nastiest looks. Said what we did off duty was our own affair, but he wasn't having us wasting time on the Unit.'

'How unreasonable!' Jean burst out indignantly.

'That's what I said,' Tony agreed. 'I told him we confined our necking to our free time. I meant it as a joke, but he hasn't much sense of humour, has he? I tell you I left his office feeling as if I'd been under a steamroller, if you know what I mean.'

Jean did know. It transpired that Tony hadn't seen fit to mention his impending divorce. 'Not his business, after all. A pity I shan't be able to drive you to London.'

She felt almost too tired to make the effort to drive herself on her next free weekend, but it was quite a time since she had seen her family. Her mother didn't miss much, for all her children's conviction that she couldn't be bothered with their problems.

'You're looking peaky, Jean—any reason?'

'Overwork,' said Jean. They were alone on the terrace on Sunday morning with a pre-lunch drink, waiting for the rest of the family to join them.

She stared into her glass and her mother went on, 'Tom thought you had something on your mind. That you seemed rather tense. Darling, I've never been one to probe——'

'Then don't start now.' Jean swallowed her drink in one mouthful and walked into the house quickly, perilously close to tears.

The weekend, that she had thought would be a welcome respite, had turned into a weary counting of the hours until Monday morning, when she would see Alex again. She returned earlier than usual with a ridiculous half hope that he might have come in to see someone, and that she might meet him in Sister's office.

Liz was there, looking blooming. She was disinclined to talk much about Tom, and Jean understood and sympathised. She knew that her brother telephoned regularly and that Liz was going down to London on her next days off duty.

Alex didn't come and after hanging around hopelessly, she went to bed later than she usually did when she was off duty. Monday was a gruelling day, made worse by the fact that Pollock was away. Alex announced that Tony was to work in number two theatre with Peter, while he and Jean would occupy number one. She stood beside him, scrubbing up, and hoped that he was in a reasonably good mood.

'It's going to be a little tricky managing an arthroplasty with just one assistant,' he said. 'I hope you're feeling strong!'

He held his hands under the drying machine, jerked his head impatiently at her to hurry up and strode into Theatre. She was nervous because she was afraid of doing something wrong. Usually Tony was first assistant for the big cases. When they had finished and were slipping off their gloves, she apologised for being ham-fisted.

'I haven't done many arthroplasties. Perhaps you'd have been better with Peter.'

He tugged his mask off and wiped the sweat from his forehead. 'And you with Wilson? I thought I'd made it plain that the less you two are together on duty the better?'

'You've made it quite plain,' she said tensely, 'and it wasn't necessary. For goodness' sake, do you think Tony and I fool around during operations?'

'No, I assume even you two have some sense of propriety, but women are so emotional. They can't keep their minds on their work in the way men can.' He looked down at her with open dislike. 'I'll tell you one thing, Miss Muir, you're the last girl I'll have on my unit for a long, long time.'

'You've always had girls on the Unit,' Jean retorted, stung to pertness by his unfairness. 'What about the nurses, not to mention physiotherapists, secretaries and——'

He held up his hand, his face grim. 'They're different. Our relationship with them isn't so close. I'm not responsible for disciplining them, thank God.'

'But——'

'Stop arguing,' he said under his breath. 'Why do you always have to have the last word?'

'Because you're so unreasonable,' she whispered to his departing back. She slipped out of her theatre boots, shrugged into her white coat and raced along to the residents' quarters for coffee. When she returned, breathless, ten minutes later, the others were just coming out of the surgeons' room.

'I poured coffee for you,' said Peter.

'I won't bother, thanks.'

She trailed back into Theatre behind her chief.

'Trouble on the wards, Miss Muir?' he asked.

'Not really.'

When they stopped for lunch she was slipping away again, but he called her back. They stood for a few seconds, looking at each other down the length of the theatre corridor.

'Yes?' Jean asked resentfully.

Alex beckoned, frowning, and she walked slowly back to his side.

'Where are you off to?'

'I have some things to do.'

'What exactly?'

'Oh, nothing important.'

'Then if it's not important it can wait,' he said sharply. 'You've not eaten since breakfast. I don't want you passing out on me in the middle of the list.'

She chewed her way through the usual uninspiring hospital sandwiches, swallowed indifferent coffee and contributed nothing to the conversation. The afternoon list dragged on without any untoward incidents, and at five-thirty they were getting to the end of the last case.

Alex, meticulously stitching tendons together, asked Jean if she knew how the patient had cut them.

'He put his hand through a glass window, poor boy.'

'Yes, I know, but did he tell you why?'

The young man had only come into hospital on the previous day, and Jean hadn't had time to do more than check his fitness for operation. She shook her head.

'He got back from work one day to find the house locked up. When he went round to the back door there was his mother lying with her head in the gas oven. So he put his fist through the window and severed half his tendons, the radial artery and the ulnar nerve. He'd nearly bled to death before a neighbour came.'

'And his mother?'

'Dead. Her marriage was disintegrating and she couldn't take it.' He stressed that fact quite deliberately, and she knew he was reminding her that women cared about losing their men. She wondered for a moment if Tony's wife cared, and while she was thinking about this he went on.

'A sad story, don't you think? This lad was an apprentice tool-maker, and I doubt if he'll ever have a normal right hand again. If he recovers fifty per cent function he'll be lucky.'

'Why wasn't he under us when he first had the injury?' Jean asked, and Alex explained that he came from another town.

'It's usual, as you know, to repair flexor tendons after the original injury has healed. Barrington, whom he was originally under, sent him to me, because he knows I'm interested in hand injuries.'

He said it casually, but Jean knew that he was the authority in this part of England on this particular problem. They had a weekly hand clinic and he was forever dinning into his juniors the vital importance of never treating any hand injury lightly.

'Incorrect assessment could mean that a man's whole working life is at stake,' he had said on one occasion.

'Could this boy go on with his old job without full use of his hands?' Jean asked.

'Doubtful. He'll probably have to go to a rehabilitation centre and train for a new job, unless we're very lucky.'

'If anyone can do it you can.' She spoke without thinking, and his eyebrows went up.

'What touching faith, Miss Muir. And very unexpected!'

She felt her cheeks go warm under her mask, but was spared the need of replying when the theatre doors swung open and Pollock looked in, careful not to cross the yellow line on the floor. He was obviously very pleased with himself.

'Hey, Alex! Good news. I've got it!'

Alex stitched and tied before he turned his head. 'Splendid, that's the best news I've heard in ages, John. Miss Muir, you can finish this off, can't you? I want to talk to Pollock.'

Inevitably Jean was a little slower in sewing up the wound than Alex would have been. By the time she left Theatre the door of the surgeons' room was shut, which meant that the men were changing. She heard voices and laughter from inside and it dawned on her now that Pollock must have been for another interview, and presumably a successful one.

Peter filled in the details later. 'It's a consultant post in the North, near the Lake District. John Pollock's charmed at the idea of living up there. Says he's never liked the Midlands anyway.'

'I'm so glad for him,' Jean said sincerely. 'I began to think he would never make it.'

'So did we all. But Tony had it on the grapevine that Mackenzie worked very hard on his behalf. We're all going round to Pollock's house for a celebration.'

'We can't all go,' Jean demurred. 'I'm off, but you're not. But I don't feel in a party mood, so I'll willingly stand in for you.'

'No need. The boss says we can all go, but those on duty are to limit themselves to one glass of champagne!'

The entire Pollock family seemed to be in a state of euphoria. The residents who had been invited walked round to the house, a modest semi-detached in a side road near the hospital, and Mrs Pollock greeted them happily at the front door. Jean she kissed on the cheek, an unusual act for a woman so reserved, and Jean responded with a warm hug.

'We're all delighted for you, Mrs Pollock. We shall miss your husband, of course.'

The living-room was already crammed with doctors, nurses, radiographers, physiotherapists, in fact all the people Pollock had got to know in his long years as a registrar at the Royal. He moved among them filling up their glasses. One of the medical registrars was opening another bottle of champagne, and as the cork popped and the wine fizzed out there were cheers and laughter.

'Should have put it in the fridge,' someone said, and Pollock, looking a different man from the dour individual of the last few months, smiled broadly.

'No room, old chap. More where that came from!'

Jean, whose legs ached after a long day standing in Theatre, perched on the arm of the sofa next to the older of Pollock's two boys. He was a quiet youngster, who seemed a little overwhelmed by the noise and excitement. Jean knew him slightly, and he seemed relieved to have her next to him. He told her that of course he was glad for Dad's sake, but he was going to miss his mates at school.

'There'll be compensations,' Jean pointed out. 'You can go on adventure courses in the mountains.'

He looked interested and she was just about to tell him of the trips her brothers had made, when there was a commotion at the door and in walked Alexander Mackenzie accompanied by Pauline Chalmers. Jean wasn't surprised to see Alex. The other orthopaedic consultant was already there, but Pauline seemed out of place, looked it too, being rather overdressed for the casual style of the celebration.

Pollock squeezed his way through the tightly packed crowd to greet his chief, who said pleasantly, 'Pauline couldn't remember if she's met you, John. We had something fixed for this evening, so I knew you wouldn't mind my bringing her.'

Pollock's eyes were fixed on Pauline's low-cut dress in a slightly dazed way. 'Er—yes—we have just met,' he murmured, and Pauline's clear voice carried above the general hubbub.

'I always feel at such a disadvantage with all you dedicated medicals!'

And that was an untruth, Jean thought with unusual cattiness. The other girl had more than her share of self-assurance.

'Who's that phoney girl talking to Dad?' young Keith Pollock asked.

'Hush!' Jean reproved, though she felt more like hugging him. 'She's a friend of Mr Mackenzie's.'

'Funny sort of friend for someone like him,' Keith said, puzzled. Fortunately this rather indiscreet conversation was interrupted by Keith's mother, gesticulating from the doorway.

'Come and help,' she called, and Jean decided to go too.

Mrs Pollock, harassed but happy, was trying to turn out plates of sandwiches for her visitors. 'I hope it's adequate. If they eat nothing all that champagne will go to their heads. We can't have the entire medical staff of the Royal drunk and disorderly.' She giggled lightheartedly.

'I don't think they'll even notice what they're eating,' Jean smiled. 'I'll butter the bread and you put in the fillings. And Keith can carry them through.'

'You are a dear girl,' Nancy Pollock exclaimed, and Pollock reiterated that a few minutes later when he looked into the kitchen accompanied by Alex.

Mrs Pollock smiled rather shyly when Alex told her how pleased he was by the good news. After they had gone out again she confessed that she found him rather alarming. 'And John hasn't always got on too well with him. Though in all fairness it was a difficult situation—their both being candidates for the same job.'

'I know, but people say he tried very hard to help your husband over this job, the one he's got.'

'John knows that,' Nancy said quickly, 'and he is grateful. Me too. Do you find him—well, tough to work for?'

'Very tough,' Jean said with a sigh, and Nancy looked sympathetic.

'John says it's not really a suitable job for a girl, but you'll soon be finished, won't you?'

'Yes,' Jean said bleakly, and then Keith bounced in again.

'Break it up, Mum! They're waiting for more.'

Jean carried the last plate of sandwiches into the living-room. Quite a few people had already left, but Alex and Pauline were still there. Someone had put a record on in the dining-room, and they had pushed the furniture against the walls. A few couples were dancing and Tony pulled Jean into the room, as she stood a little irresolutely in the doorway.

'Why so glum? Get with it, girl!'

He swung her round and she responded with a gallant attempt at gaiety. The old-fashioned linoleum floor, cracked in places, didn't make dancing easy. The room was too small and there was too much furniture. She stumbled over something, and Tony caught her before she fell, pinning her for a moment againt the wall, and planting a kiss on her mouth as he did so.

Several people applauded noisily. Jean shook her hair back from her face and looked straight into Alex's contemptuous eyes. He was standing with Pauline by the door, and John Pollock was just behind them.

Defiantly she put her hands in Tony's and they joined the dancers again. The other three walked into the garden. Through the open French windows she could see John Pollock showing Alex his roses.

Pauline, looking bored, drifted back into the room. Jean's one desire was to get away before the others returned.

'I'm feeling tired, Tony. Why don't you dance with Pauline?'

She slipped out of his arms and made for the door. The kitchen was empty, so she went in and sat on one of the stools, resting her elbows on the work top. 'I'll go back to the hospital soon,' she thought, but she didn't as yet feel up to making the effort. A powerful lethargy had overcome her, which had its roots in the bitterness of knowing that Alex despised her.

There was a sound behind her and she swung round as Alex spoke. 'All alone, Miss Muir? I thought you were such a popular girl.'

'I have to go,' she said, sliding off the stool on curiously wobbly legs.

He pushed the door to and gave her an unpleasant smile. 'Not just yet. I have something to say to you.'

He blocked the doorway and she could hardly push him out of the way without an undignified and ridiculous scuffle.

'This is supposed to be a celebration,' she said wearily. 'Don't you think you could leave it till tomorrow?'

'No, I don't.' He advanced into the room, his anger barely suppressed. 'What a little cheat you are! You can't pretend now that you don't know Tony's married.'

'He's getting a divorce,' Jean said, and he gave a scornful laugh.

'So that makes it all right! You break up a marriage——'

'The divorce had nothing to do with me——'

'I find that hard to believe.'

'I don't care what you believe!' She was as angry as him now, and spoke a little wildly. 'It has nothing to do with you anyway.'

'No, it hasn't, I suppose,' he agreed, 'except that I was sorry for you once when I thought he was making a fool of you. Now I realise I was the fool. You're the sort of girl who enjoys her power over men.' He leant against the work counter, his dark face twisted and cynical. 'Little Miss Muir, the girl everyone likes and wants to help. Sir Geoffrey and John Pollock—oh, and Sefton, I mustn't forget him—they all think you're a sweet kid, though God knows why. But I don't like you, my dear, and I certainly don't want to help you! And if you were serious about wanting that dermatology post at the Royal, I shall do my best to see that you don't get it.'

Her anger had gone now, to be replaced by a desolate aching unhappiness. 'Please go away,' she whispered. 'You've made your point.'

It seemed that he wanted to inflict as much hurt as he could. 'You're a disruptive influence in the Royal, Miss Muir,' he went on relentlessly. 'I suppose I shall have to give you a reference, since your work is quite good, but I shall certainly make it plain that you're not a desirable colleague.'

'I wouldn't ask you for a reference if my career depended on it!' she cried, and then mercifully someone pushed the door open and she rushed out.

The hall was full of people, so it was easy to escape without being noticed. Jean walked fast, the tears brimming over, brushing them away with the back of her hand. She turned left instead of right, because she couldn't go back to the hospital until she'd recovered her composure.

She came to a small, sad-looking square with worn grass and a few plane trees. There was a bench, so she sat down and stared at some children on bicycles.

Peter's voice came from behind her. 'Jean love, what's wrong? You looked awful when you were leaving.' He sat down on the other end of the bench. 'Can I help?'

He was a gentle, kindly young man and a good friend. 'You could lend me a hanky,' Jean said, with a shaky sort of laugh. 'Where's Della?'

Della was his girl-friend, who had also been at the party.

'She went back with the pysio girls. She told me to come and see if you were all right.'

'You're lucky to have Della,' Jean said wistfully.

'I know it, but we're talking about you.'

'I suppose I've made a complete fool of myself?' She wiped her eyes and blew her nose. 'Did everybody see?'

'I'm sure they didn't. Probably only Della and me, because you rushed right past us. Was it—anything to do with Mackenzie?'

'Why do you ask that?' she parried, and he frowned and stared down at his feet.

'Because I saw him in the kitchen and I know he gets under your skin.'

Peter was to be trusted, and it did help sometimes to talk. 'We had a row.' She rubbed her aching eyes. 'It was a—a shock to discover just how much he dislikes me.'

'And you?'

'I what?'

'Do you dislike him?'

She looked away, over the unattractive little square and the dusty flowers, sighed and shook her head. 'If I had an atom of sense I should, but I don't, Peter. I love him, and—and I'm so unhappy.' She blew her nose again. 'I'm all right now. Let's go back to the hospital.'

# CHAPTER TWELVE

One good thing about a demanding job like surgery was that it left very little time for brooding. During working hours Jean made a great effort, and managed to keep her problems at bay. Nights were bad though, and after a strenuous day she needed a good sleep. In the past, before she had fallen in love, she could go to sleep in a few minutes. Now she stayed up late, whether she was on duty or off, rather than face those tormented wakeful hours.

One night, when all the other residents had gone to bed, Liz, coming back into the Night Sisters' office, gave her a disapproving look.

'Still up? I thought you were off duty.'

'I'm just going, Liz. Give me a couple of sleeping pills. Anything will do.'

Liz stared. 'Whatever for? I don't approve of the patients having them, let alone the staff.'

'Don't be so stuffy!' Jean snapped. 'If you won't give me them, I shall simply go to the dispensary and collect them for myself.'

'All right!' Liz spoke nearly as sharply. 'No need to bite my head off. Here you are.' She shook a couple of pink pills into her palm from one of the bottles on her tray. 'Guaranteed to knock you out for a few hours. One will probably be enough, though, if you're not used to them.'

Perhaps one would have been enough, but Jean craved for a deep untroubled sleep. She did indeed have that, but she woke late feeling sluggish and confused, and realised with dismay that this wasn't the best day to have a hangover.

She drank two cups of black coffee, liberally sweetened, nibbled a piece of toast and reached the front hall just as

Alex walked in for the start of his ward round. She kept well to the back for most of the time, except when Alex asked her a direct question about one of the patients. She had never taken barbiturates before and hadn't realised that they could have this effect on some people. She gave her head a little shake and rubbed her forehead hard, then blushed as she caught Alex's eyes on her.

'Is something wrong, Miss Muir? Feeling unwell?'

'I have a headache.'

They were just about to move on from the men's to the women's ward. 'Sit down for a minute or two,' he suggested quite kindly. 'You can join us again if you feel better.'

So she sat in Sister's office, swallowed a couple of aspirins and shut her eyes. Sister, a friendly soul, advised her to go and lie on her bed.

'You look awful, Dr Muir.'

'I'll be all right,' Jean murmured, and shortly afterwards she set off to find the others.

She saw them disappearing down the main corridor in the direction of the children's ward. She hesitated outside the door that led to the resident's quarters, half minded to take Sister's advice, but she was very keen to hear what Alex thought about Jamie Martin's progress.

Jamie had been admitted last week after the go-kart he was riding with another boy had careered down a hill into a bus. The other child had been killed instantly. Jamie, they hoped, was lucky to be alive—would be lucky, at least, if he had no permanent brain damage and wasn't too badly crippled.

Jean had helped her chief the evening he had picked pieces of skull bone out of Jamie's brain, and repaired his broken limbs. She had sat up for what was left of that night, coping with his routine resuscitation. Yesterday Jamie had at last been pronounced out of danger and moved from the Intensive Care Unit to the children's ward, where they hoped he would be happier.

He was in a side ward, where it was quiet, but as soon as he was fit enough they planned to move him into the main ward. He was nine years old, a sturdy little boy with a pale face smothered in freckles, and carroty hair. His parents spent as much time as they could with him, but his father worked long hours and his mother had to look after Jamie's three younger sisters.

'I can't neglect them,' she had told Jean tearfully the other day. 'We're new here, you see, and don't know many people. Haven't got any relatives either in the area.'

So the nurses mothered him when his real mother wasn't around, and Jean too, when she could spare the time. Now she stood just inside the glass door of Jamie's room and listened to Alex talking to the child.

The little boy watched Alex with the grave intent stare that was difficult to interpret. Was he slow to understand because of his brain injuries, or did he always look like that? Today he seemed fretful, more irritable than he usually was.

'That isn't necessarily a bad sign,' Alex pointed out. 'It may mean that he's more aware of the external world, and that he finds it exhausting. So absolute quite, please, Sister, and close observation, of course.'

They broke up outside the door of the children's ward, but Alex beckoned to Jean. 'Feeling better?' He subjected her to a thorough scrutiny. 'You haven't looked yourself lately. Any reason?'

'Not really.' She avoided his eyes, anxious to be off.

'Headache gone?'

'Almost, but that was due to sleeping pills.' The moment the words were out she regretted them.

'Sleeping pills? A healthy young woman shouldn't need them. Getting neurotic, Miss Muir?'

'I don't usually take then,' she muttered. 'But—but it's been rather noisy the last few nights,' she improvised, and made a move to leave him.

He caught her by the coat sleeve. 'Don't rush off, I haven't finished. You have me worried now, my girl.'

Was he interested enough to be worried? Perhaps the thought showed on her face, because he gave her arm a slight shake.

'Don't start playing about with pills, little one. There are quite a few cases of young doctors getting hooked on barbiturates or whatever.'

'Honestly! I take them for the first time in my life and you and Liz act as if I'm turning into a drug addict!'

'So Sister Davies keeps an eye on you, does she? Sensible girl, that! May I inquire whether her romance is prospering?'

'I suppose so. She doesn't discuss it.'

'Wise girl. And yours, Miss Muir? Could it be that you're not as sure of Tony Wilson as you'd like to be? Could that be why you're not sleeping?'

He looked down at her very intently, and although she resented his questions they were put quite gently, as if he was genuinely concerned about her.

'I have got problems,' she answered, low-voiced, 'but I don't want to talk about them. Not to you, anyway.'

'Fair enough,' he said briskly, with a return to his usual manner. As they walked down the corridor in the direction of the dining-room he added, 'Keep an eye on Jamie for the next twenty-four hours. Irritability could be a sign of another bleed into his brain.'

So last thing at night, after she had seen all the other patients she went along to the little boy. He was sleeping quietly now, his dirty worn old teddy bear clutched in his arms. Jean bent over him with the nurse and tears filled her eyes.

'I do hope he'll make it,' she whispered, and blew her nose rather shamefacedly. 'I know it's silly to get worked up, but there's something so—so vulnerable about a sleeping child, isn't there?'

The other girl nodded sympathetically. 'It kind of gets you, doesn't it? Don't worry, Doctor, we'll keep a sharp eye on him, though we are terribly short-staffed tonight.'

That was nothing new. Hardly a hospital in the country had their full quota of nurses. 'Call on me if you need an extra pair of hands,' Jean said, and went back to the residents' quarters.

She was on call tonight and half expected to be roused again for any one of half a dozen patients. So she didn't undress completely, but slipped into bed after removing her blouse and skirt. Rather to her surprise she wasn't called, and even without sleeping pills had a very good night.

She did a quick round of her more worrying patients before the fracture clinic. Jamie, eyes sunken in his small pale face, felt like talking. Clutching her hand, he made her promise to come back that afternoon.

'Me mum can't come. She has to take the little ones to the clinic. An' I want to hear the end of the story.'

'What story?'

'The one he read last night when I couldn't sleep. The nice doctor, you know.'

'You were asleep when I did my night round.'

'I woke up again. I had a horrid dream.'

Tony had been on duty with her, and Jean was touched by this kind behaviour.

'Doctor Wilson?' she asked, and he nodded. 'The nice one,' he murmured rather drowsily, so she gave his hand a little squeeze.

'Off to sleep, Jamie. You'll need it if you were awake in the night. I promise I'll be back later.'

It was her half day, but she had nothing special planned. She needed a shampoo and some make-up, a new pair of shoes, perhaps. Tony wasn't free, and she hadn't fixed anything up with any of the others. To pass the time she went to a film, and returned to the hospital around eleven.

Meeting Liz near the porter's lodge she said impulsively,

'I've been meaning to say sorry. You know, for snapping the other night.'

Liz smiled. 'Forget it, but it's so unlike you, Jean. What had upset you?' Her nice honest face was puckered with worry. 'I've noticed a change in you lately. Anything I can do to help?'

'No, Liz, but thank you.'

'Come and have a cuppa. Oh, come on, Jean, you always do.'

Rather reluctantly she accompanied Liz to the office, which was more crowded than usual, so that she had to lean against the wall.

'Have my chair.' Alex, who was engaged in a conversation with Tony, stood up. Tony didn't appear to have noticed her till now, but he jumped up as well.

'Have mine.'

'I'm not that decrepit——' but Alex put a firm hand on her shoulder and she sat down meekly.

He was discussing one of the patients he had operated on yesterday. Jean listened and when they had finished, and Alex had turned away for a word with Liz, she leant towards Tony.

'It was terribly kind of you, sitting up with Jamie last night.'

He stared. 'What are you on about?'

'Your reading to Jamie because he couldn't get to sleep. It must have been all hours before you were in bed.'

'I didn't read to the brat. In my opinion he's outrageously spoilt. And I don't like children, anyway.'

'But he said——'

Liz joined in. 'It was Mr Mackenzie, Jean.' She gave the surgeon a warm smile, and he looked rather put out.

'The child was restless, Miss Muir, and the nurses were too busy to sit with him.' He rose abruptly. 'Good night, everyone.'

Jean looked after him and sighed. What a complex character he had! He was sharp-tongued, a tough disciplinarian, but he could be heartwarmingly human on occasion. Far kinder really than Tony, who couldn't be bothered with a difficult child. More worth loving in fact, though one didn't, she had found, choose whom one loved. She had disliked him heartily at first—still did sometimes.

'Cheer up,' Tony murmured in her ear. 'You'll see him again tomorrow.'

She went red, then white, and jumped up as abruptly as Alex had. She was halfway down the corridor before Tony caught up with her.

'Hang on, Jean. No need to take off like that!'

There was no one around at the moment. The enormous corridor spread before and behind them, the lights dimmed for night time.

Jean said angrily, 'I don't care for that sort of joke.'

Tony's handsome face was rueful. 'It wasn't really intended as a joke, love. But I'm sorry I spoke. Honestly.'

She looked down at her hands. 'Is it so obvious? I suppose half the hospital knows?'

'Of course not. Only the people who know you really well, and have noticed the change in you since he came back. Besides, I'm not a complete fool. You're on edge when he's around, you put on a terrific act with me——'

'Oh, Tony!' She felt ashamed of herself. 'You make me feel a real phoney.'

He took her arm and walked her off down the corridor. 'I don't know anyone who's less of a phoney than you. Let's find somewhere a little more private.'

There were still a few people in the residents' sitting-room, but the kitchen was empty. Tony plugged the electric kettle in and busied himself making coffee. 'Want to talk about it?'

Jean laughed, with a touch of hysteria. 'Honestly, it has its funny side. Only a few nights ago I was crying on Peter's shoulder. I'm beginning to think that the sooner I leave here the better.'

Tony put a cup of coffee into her hand and stirred his own vigorously. 'I think so too. He's not for you, Jean, though you may think you want him.'

'You don't have to rub it in. I know there's Pauline.'

'Pauline!' He dismissed her with a scornful flick of the fingers. 'A man like our Alex couldn't be seriously interested in that bird-brain. I'd say he's simply not the marrying kind. Too self-contained, a loner—you know.'

Alex had more or less said the same thing, when he was telling her about his difficult childhood. She sighed, drank her coffee far too hot, and burnt her tongue.

'I do know,' she said sadly. 'I don't kid myself I have any chance with him. He's as good as told me he'll be glad when I go. You're not annoyed because I—well, I sort of used you?' She coloured as she remembered the way she had allowed him to make love to her.

Tony's smile was quite spontaneous. 'Available any time, that's me. Every girl's antidote to a love affair gone wrong.'

He would joke about it, of course. He was made that way.

'Oh, Tony——'

'Don't go on about it, Jean. We both enjoyed ourselves—at least I did. Even though I always had the idea I was only a substitute.'

She put her cup down. 'I think I'll go to bed. I'm awfully tired. You've been very understanding, Tony.'

He gave her a sympathetic grin. 'That's because I've been through it myself. I know what it's like, eating your heart out for someone. And I went a lot further than you did. I didn't just fool around with some other girl, I got married.'

Jean had another sleepless night, worrying away at the thought that she might be making a fool of herself. Tony had implied that her feelings for Alex were only obvious to her close friends. She hoped that was true, because she knew how uncharitable hospital gossip could be. It it reached Alex—or if he had the faintest suspicion how she felt—her cheeks burned at the thought. But surely her behavior with Tony had put him off that idea? And so her thoughts went round and round, until at last she fell asleep.

In the morning, when she wakened, she picked up her diary and looked at the calendar. July the twenty-second. Just about six more weeks before she was due to leave the Royal. No, less, because she had two weeks' leave owing to her, which the junior doctors usually took at the end of each six months' session.

So a month to get through as best she could, and the best way was to work even harder. Perhaps some project? She asked Pollock's advice, and he suggested a series on ankle injuries not involving fractures. It didn't sound very inspiring, but he pointed out that it was a rather neglected subject, and wouldn't be too difficult for a beginner.

'And good practice if you want to learn how to write papers. I didn't know you had ambitions in that direction.'

'I haven't really, but I feel I've got to keep my end up with my brothers,' she joked. 'They're always publishing papers in the medical journals.'

So in her free time, instead of sitting around playing bridge, or gossiping with the others, Jean sifted through casualty cards and ward notes for the cases that interested her. One evening she was in the Records department, putting files away in the sliding shelves when the doors swung to, and Alex strode in, looking annoyed.

'Why the devil don't you tell switchboard when you hide away somewhere?'

'I did tell them. They must have forgotten.'

He gave her a disbelieving look. 'I've a case lined up for eleven-thirty. A circular saw injury, very nasty. Why do people have to use circular saws at this hour? And for that matter, why are you working so late, Miss Muir?'

He bent over the desk where she had been working. She slammed the heavy metal shelves back into place and came quickly over.

'Just making some notes.' She snatched them up, afraid he would laugh at her efforts.

'Why the secrecy?'

She clutched them to her rather defensively. 'No secret, but it wouldn't interest you. I thought it would be fun to try and write a paper, and Pollock suggested a subject.'

'Let's have a look.' He held out a hand.

'I'll show you when it's finished. I should just about get it done before—before I leave.' Her voice quavered slightly and he frowned.

'You finished next month, don't you? I've been meaning to talk to you about that for some time. Made any plans yet?'

The thought of leaving the Royal was almost too painful to contemplate. 'No,' she said bleakly.

He walked up and down a couple of times as if he didn't know how to start. 'What about that dermatology job?' he asked at last.

'I've decided not to apply.'

'Why?'

'You know quite well why. You told me you'd make sure I didn't get it.'

'I shouldn't have said that.' She wondered if she had misheard him. 'One should never allow one's personal feelings to interfere with one's judgement.' He gave her a curious little half smile. 'You and Peter have been a good pair. Of course I'll back you, Jean, if you want it.'

She went on staring at him. 'Well?' he asked impatiently, but she found it hard to think clearly.

'I—I'm not sure.'

'A rest cure after the Trauma Unit,' he suggested. 'Skin patients rarely get you out of bed at night! And not a bad line for a woman to specialise in, come to think of it.'

'Why? Because it's easier than surgery?'

'You always assume I'm trying to get at you, my dear girl! Skin diseases are an extremely complicated subject. No, I meant physically easier, especially for a married woman.'

'I'll think about it,' she said uncertainly, and his good humour began to evaporate.

'You'll be very silly if you don't apply. It's easier getting another job in the same hospital.'

A little nettled by his manner, she answered sharply 'Dad says there are a whole lot of posts coming up at Queen's.'

'Ah yes, and Professor Muir's daughter is bound to get one.'

'I don't use my family connections,' she protested indignantly. 'After all, I could have had a first house job at Queen's, but I chose to come here.'

He smiled faintly. 'Simmer down, little one. It's not worth quarrelling about. I've always wondered, though, why you did come here.'

He leant against the desk as if he wasn't in any hurry. She told him, a little haltingly, how things had been at home, and he nodded sympathetically.

'If the rest of your family are anything like young Tom, I can see that they might be a bit overpowering.' He glanced at his watch. 'Let's go and have a drink before it's time for Theatre.'

He told her about the case as they walked along to the office, and Jean thought wistfully that he hadn't been so nice to her for weeks. Afterwards, sitting over a cup of coffee in the surgeons' room, she told him shyly that she had decided to apply for the dermatology post. He looked pleased, and Tony, who had also been assisting, flashed her a surprised look.

Later, walking back to the residents' quarters with her, he slipped his arm through hers. 'Is it wise, Jean? Go somewhere else. Forget the man. The longer you stay here, the harder you'll make it for yourself.'

'He suggested it.'

'So what has that got to do with it?' Tony asked, and she sighed.

'Please leave it, Tony. Maybe I'm being foolish, but that's my affair.'

She asked one of the orthopaedic secretaries to type out an application for the post of senior house officer in the Department of Dermatology. There were two dermatologists, one of them young and cheerful and a friend of Alex's, the other getting on to retiring age.

The younger man spoke to her one day. 'I'll be delighted to have you on our firm, Miss Muir. Alex says you've been a good worker, and he's not the easiest man to please.' His eyes twinkled and Jean smiled back, thinking how pleasant it would be to work for him.

His colleague was reputed to be a difficult old man, but anyone who had survived on the Trauma Unit could cope with a mere dermatologist! The thought amused her. She was feeling much happier these days, now that she was going to continue at the Royal. Tony's warning, that she would only be storing up unhappiness for herself, she pushed to the back of her mind.

Alex was behaving more agreeably too, and after one of his ward rounds he said to her, 'Sefton leaves today, so you'd better come and say goodbye to him. Though I don't doubt you'll be receiving an invitation to his house very soon.'

'Which I shall certainly accept,' she retorted cheekily.

'What you do outside the hospital is your own affair,' he said, his smile fading. 'And what you do in it won't be my affair much longer, thank God,' he added under his breath.

'That's not very kind.'

They had reached Sefton's door, and Alex knocked, but before he opened it he answered her. 'I don't feel particularly kindly towards you, my dear girl. I never have.'

He went in, followed by Jean. Sefton was sitting by the window in a wheelchair, with a rug over his knees. Pauline lounged on the windowsill, looking bored, but brightened when she saw Alex.

'Such a ridiculous lot of red tape before he can go,' she said petulantly. 'Can't you cut it short, darling?' She stood on tiptoe to kiss his cheek.

'No, Pauline, I can't,' Alex said firmly. 'Hospital routine has to be accepted or our records would go all to blazes.'

She pouted, then managed a smile. 'Well, there's one good thing about having the old man home, we'll be seeing you regularly, I suppose?'

Jean, who had been keeping in the background, gave an audible gasp, at the girl's lack of sensitivity. Sefton, who had been studying her, smiled sarcastically.

'Home life isn't all it's cracked up to be, is it, my dear? Still, it'll be nice to get out of this place.'

He looked remarkably well. Alex had put him on a diet, which he had accepted only after a prolonged battle. He had in the end lost over a stone, his face looked less high-coloured and his skin was clearer. Drinking less had probably helped too, Jean thought, giving him an affectionate smile, which was intercepted by Pauline.

'I shouldn't bother to stay, Dr Muir,' she said, an edge to her voice. 'I've one or two things to discuss with Alex.'

Jean gave her chief an uncertain glance, but Sefton spoke before Alex could. 'Don't be so damned rude, Pauline. Jean is an old friend of mine.'

'As if I didn't know,' Pauline said sweetly, and then, perhaps afraid that she had gone too far, added hastily, 'I didn't mean to be rude. I just thought the girl was bound to be busy.'

'Yes, I am.' Jean found it impossible to put on an act, so the words came out rather abruptly. She held out a hand to Sefton. 'Goodbye, Mr Chalmers. I hope all goes well for you.'

He kept her hand in his for quite a long time. 'Goodbye, Jean. Alex tells me you'll be staying on here, so you'll come and see me, I trust.'

'If I get the job,' Jean smiled, disengaging her hand, and Pauline's expression sharpened.

'I thought you were finishing in Westhampton.'

'No.' She couldn't resist adding, 'Alex thinks I ought to stay on.'

As she made for the door she saw Pauline's lips tighten, and Alex give a broad grin. Only when she was in the corridor did she realise that it wasn't done for a house surgeon to call her chief by his first name.

# CHAPTER THIRTEEN

THE interviews for the dermatology appointment were on a Tuesday at twelve-fifteen. Jean joined the orthopaedic ward round, but it went on later than usual, leaving her no time to go back to her room to tidy herself up.

She gave her white coat to Peter. 'Be a dear and dump it in the Mess. I must dash or I'll be late for my interview.'

Alex, having a last word with John Pollock about something, glanced round with a smile. 'You look very fetching, Miss Muir. Wouldn't you give her the job, John, if you were on the selection committee?'

Jean coloured at finding herself the centre of attention. She had picked her dress for the interview, a crisp navy cotton with white collar and cuffs, because it was smart yet fairly sober. She knew it flattered her, yet felt shy when she saw this fact mirrored in the eyes of the men.

John said with mock disapproval, 'Girls have an unfair advantage at interviews in my opinion.'

'They do if they look like Jean.' That was Tony's contribution.

Jean retorted quickly, 'It works both ways. Some consultants would never pick a girl unless the male applicants were quite hopeless.' She glanced at Alex as she said this, and he acknowledged her remark with a sardonic smile.

She excused herself and walked off to a chorus of 'Good lucks.'

The interviews were in the board room. Jean joined the other candidates in the waiting-room, and like them, cast a carefully casual eye over the opposition. Two rather hearty young men who seemed to have been at the same medical school, a solemn nervous girl with spectacles and an older man, around thirty, who had a confident look about him. In

Jean's somewhat limited experience, though, the outwardly confident one might be a mass of nerves underneath.

They were called in alphabetical order. She went in second and found the committee pleasant enough, except, rather disconcertingly, for the senior dermatologist. His reputation hadn't belied him. He asked some awkward questions about her dermatological experience, which was negligible.

'Just what I picked up at medical school,' Jean told him honestly. 'No, I've never looked after any skin patients.'

'And how many dermatology outpatients did you attend as a student?'

She thought. 'Twenty, perhaps.'

'So that you are quite inexperienced, Dr Muir?'

'Well, yes,' she agreed. 'But it's a subject one expects to learn after qualifying, isn't it?'

The junior dermatologist, with the suspicion of a smile, came to her rescue. 'I agree with Miss Muir. The average student doesn't have much opportunity to acquire great experience in medical specialities.'

'Doesn't make much effort to, you mean,' said the older man sourly, as if this were a favourite hobbyhorse of his.

No one had any more questions so she went back to the waiting-room. Jean, who had been encouraged to think that the job was hers, began to have doubts now. So it was less of a shock than it might have been when the confident man, who had had a longer interview than any of them, was called back in.

The secretary returned a few moments later to express formal sympathy at their lack of success. Jean, whom he knew quite well, he kept back a little longer.

'Bad luck, Dr Muir, but the chap who got it has already done a junior job in dermatology. The Committee felt that though you're our local candidate, he's had more experience.'

'Fair enough,' Jean agreed, and made her escape.

Sitting on her bed a few minutes later, she reviewed the situation. No chance of another job at the Royal in the near future. She had been so sure that she was going to get this one—encouraged to think so by her colleagues—that she hadn't applied for anything else. Now all the junior posts were filled for around six months. She would have to look for something else, perhaps in London. There were plenty of vacancies, but she had wanted this one.

She bit her lip hard to stop it trembling. When the telephone rang her voice was thick with the tears she hadn't shed.

'Peter? No, I didn't get it. Yes, I'm very disappointed. Sure, I'll be down in a few minutes.'

She blew her nose hard, splashed her face with cold water, and applied more make-up than usual. When she went down to the dining-room she was outwardly quite composed. Only her close friends might have noticed that she was more subdued than usual. She caught Alex's eye as she was sitting down, and flashed him a bright meaningless smile which he didn't return. On his way out he stopped for a moment and touched her shoulder.

'Sorry, Jean. I thought you were going to get it. You finish in ten days, don't you?'

She nodded, afraid that if she spoke her voice would betray how upset she was.

'Any other jobs in mind?'

She shook her head and took a gulp of coffee, longing for him to go away, and after a sharply speculative look at her he did.

Liz, wrapped in her own private happiness after a weekend with Tom, was inclined to think her friend's failure a blessing in disguise.

'Your family will be pleased to have you nearer home. They're a fabulous lot, Jean. You're lucky to be one of them.'

'Yes, I suppose so.'

Why was it that happiness tended to make one less sensitive? Liz was a dear and it looked as if things were working out well for her, and Jean could think of no one she would rather have for a sister-in-law, but the close friendship that had been developing between them seemed to have been nipped in the bud. They no longer gossiped together or discussed interesting cases. Liz lived now for Tom's telephone calls, and when she was with Jean wanted to hear stories about his boyhood.

Jean was due to leave on the Friday of the week following her interview. The man who was replacing her was moving to the Trauma Unit from another post at the Royal. Several other residents were leaving at the same time, so there was to be a farewell party for them all.

She would have liked to skip it, but couldn't think of a convincing excuse. So she went out on her last half day and bought herself a new dress, a trendy affair from the smartest local boutique. She washed her hair that evening. Later she put the dress on and stood in front of the mirror.

The sales girl for once had been speaking the truth. It did do something for her. Jean gave an insincere plastic smile at the dazzling girl in the glass, tore the dress off and threw herself on the bed in tears.

Thursday was her last working day. John Pollock commented on this in Theatre while they were waiting between cases. He himself had another few weeks to go before he took up his new appointment.

'You don't like changes, do you, Alex? Before long you and Tony will be the only ones of the old team left.'

Peter finished a month after Jean. He already had a post fixed up in psychiatry and was planning to marry his girlfriend. Jean thought sadly that everyone else was looking forward to the future. For her it stretched bleakly ahead, and the most she could look forward to was a gradual blunting of unhappiness.

'Why so glum, little one?' Alex asked, coming to stand beside her. 'Can it be that you're sorry to be leaving?'

He held his gloved hands lightly clasped in front of him. His thick dark eyebrows, so striking above the white mask, were raised questioningly. She was glad that her own mask concealed most of her face.

'It's always a bit of a wrench leaving any place,' she parried. 'I felt the same when I finished after five years at medical school.'

He leant against the wall beside her. 'You leave at the weekend?'

'No, tomorrow. Are you coming to our farewell party?' She was proud of the casual way she managed that.

'I may not be able to.' He didn't sound very interested, and indeed why should he be? Consultants occasionally turned up at their juniors' parties, out of a sense of duty, mostly.

'After all, they don't invite us to theirs,' Peter had pointed out, when the residents were discussing which of their chiefs were least likely to dampen down the proceedings.

Jean was very quiet for the rest of the list, wrote her operation notes up quickly and went along to the wards. She was on duty this evening, so she might not spend much time at the party anyway. She certainly wouldn't be able to drink much, which was a pity, because alcohol might at least have given her morale a boost.

She wanted to say goodbye to one or two of her favourite patients, young Jamie, now well on the way to recovery, and old Mark Thompson, who hadn't in the end been fit enough for the outing she had planned for him.

'I'll miss you, Doctor,' he said, his thin voice even more quavery than usual. 'Do you have to go? Don't you like it here?'

Jean tried to explain that six months was the usual length of the junior doctors' appointments, but he gave a disapproving grunt.

'Seems daft to me. Just when you're getting the hang of

things they move you on.' He looked over her shoulder. 'Isn't that so, sir?'

Jean turned, to find Alex behind her, a faint smile on his face. 'Just saying goodbye to a few old friends,' she murmured, and he nodded and stood waiting. 'Do you want me for something?'

'No hurry, Miss Muir. Going to miss her, Thompson?'

'I am that,' the old man said wistfully. 'But perhaps she'll come back to see us, sir?'

'I'm not sure she likes us enough for that,' the surgeon said drily.

Jean gave Mr Thompson's hand a squeeze. 'If I do come back, and you're well enough, I won't forget that outing.'

The old man's face registered quite plainly his feelings. He knew as well as they did that he wouldn't be going anywhere ever again, but if they wanted to maintain the fiction that he would, then he would play along with them.

'He knows he won't get better, doesn't he?' she murmured, as they left the ward.

Alex nodded, his face sombre. 'The only consolation is that he doesn't much care. After all, where would he go? Who would look after him? The real tragedy is when a youngish man with a wife and family dies, after some accident that nine times out of ten could have been avoided. Or some dearly loved child. After twelve years of surgery I still find it difficult to accept a child's death.'

He dug his hands into his pockets as if ashamed to admit to his feelings, and walked along at his usual cracking pace. Outside his office he stopped.

'Come in for a moment, Jean. Sit down. You look tired —or is it unhappy?' he added softly.

'It was a long list. What did you want to see me about? I've been through all the ward notes——'

'Forget about the patients for five minutes!' he snapped. 'You're becoming quite obsessional about your work.'

'I don't like leaving things in a muddle.'

'Argumentative to the end, aren't you? Sit down,' he said again. He looked down at the papers on his desk, then up at her, with a frown. 'I'm not blind, my dear, nor as insensitive as you seem to think. I know quite well that you're not happy. Care to talk about it?'

He was watching her steadily. She sat down because it was something to do, and stared with bent head at her hands. 'No, I wouldn't,' she whispered, and two tears rolled down her cheeks.

'Oh, God!' he said furiously, under his breath. He felt for a handkerchief and passed it to her. 'Westhampton isn't that far from London,' he observed.

Jean wiped her eyes and gazed at him dumbly. Had he guessed how she felt? Was he trying to be kind?

'He used to go to London to visit his wife. So now he'll be visiting you.' His mouth twisted in the cynical smile she didn't like. 'So what's wrong? Can't trust him to be faithful when you're not around?'

She understood at last. 'Tony!' she exclaimed incredulously. 'You think I'm unhappy about Tony!' She started to laugh hysterically and then found to her dismay that she couldn't stop.

Alex stared at her, puzzled at first, and then with growing concern. 'Jean, don't.' He came to her side, bent down and put his hands on her shoulders. 'What the devil is wrong with you?' He gave her a hard shake.

She sobered as quickly as she had lost control, and sat quite still. His hands gripped her shoulders, his face was close to hers, anxious, uncertain—and very dear.

'I'm all right now,' she whispered. 'Please leave me alone.'

She stood up, and although he straightened too, he didn't move away. They stood very close, looking at each other. Jean knew that she must go before she made a complete fool of herself, only—this might be the last time she would ever be alone with him.

She gave a little despairing sigh and saw comprehension and incredulity dawn on his face. The thing she had dreaded above everything else had happened.

She stammered, 'I have to go—the party——'

'No!' he said sharply. 'Jean——'

There was a rap on the door and she turned thankfully. His secretary came in with a sheaf of letters for him to sign, leaving the door open behind her.

Jean slipped out quickly, ignoring his call to stop, and raced down the corridor to the residents' quarters. She didn't want kind platitudes. She didn't want him to feel embarrassed or awkward because a foolish girl, who had started by disliking him, had ended by falling madly in love with him.

She ran a bath but stayed in it for only a few minutes, because she was on call, and even doctors didn't have a telephone in the bathroom. Then she pulled on the new dress and did her hair, fixing it on the nape of her neck with a silver clasp her mother had given her.

She was quite calm now. It was almost a relief not to have to put on an act any more. She was quite sure he wouldn't come to the party, and with any luck they would get through the night without meeting again. John Pollock was on call too, and only for a major accident would he summon his chief.

Jean went down to supper a few minutes later with her face carefully made up, to hide the traces of the emotional storm she had been through. Peter gave her a sharp glance, and another of the residents whistled admiringly.

'You look fabulous, Jean! My girl never seems to find gear like that.'

'It's not the dress. It's who's inside it,' one of the house physicians said, amid laughter, and Jean laughed too, but wondered why she couldn't have had the sense to fall in love with one of them. A lot of them weren't married. She had been out with several of them in the past and enjoyed their company, in the happy uncomplicated days before Alex had returned.

Supper was eaten more quickly than usual because they wanted to get ahead with preparations for the party. Tony was the Mess president and had organised the drinks and snacks very efficiently. The girls were recruited to lay out bowls of crisps and other savouries. Jean was carrying several bowls along when she bumped into John Pollock and his wife on the stairs.

'Hey, that looks dangerous!' He rescued several bowls before they toppled. 'But I don't think you're going to eat many of them. I've just accepted three emergencies from outside our area. The emergency bed service say the hospital they should have gone to is bursting at the seams.'

'I don't feel in the party mood anyhow,' said Jean. She glanced at her watch. 'How soon will they be here?'

'About half an hour. I've asked the wards to notify us as soon as they arrive.'

Mrs Pollock subsided on a sofa. 'Sit down, Jean. You may be on your feet half the night.'

She had been a Theatre Sister when she married John Pollock, so she knew, none better, the sort of life they led. Jean sat down willingly and stayed beside her while people drifted in, and the party warmed up. Peter brought her a small gin and tonic.

'More tonic than gin,' he apologised, 'but the boss doesn't approve of drinking on duty, and quite right too.'

'Here's to you, Jean,' said Nancy Pollock. 'I hope you find a nice job soon.'

The noise was becoming deafening and Jean wasn't sorry when the telephone rang to summon them to the wards. John Pollock looked the new admissions over with her, and decided to operate as soon as possible. They had all been in one car and were lucky to be alive, for the occupants of the other car had been killed instantly.

'Check on their general condition,' said John, 'while I fix

Theatre up.'

He disappeared into Sister's office. Jean was just removing the blood pressure cuff from the last patient when he returned with Alex. He had apparently decided that speed was important and that it would be better to run two theatres. Alex, after a rapid examination, agreed.

'We'll need another pair of hands. Is young Davidson around?'

'He's at the party,' said John Pollock.

'Ah, yes, your farewell party, Jean.' Alex looked her over, taking in the gay dress underneath her white coat. 'Sorry to spoil your fun.'

She swallowed hard and avoided his eyes. 'I'll ring Peter,' she murmured, thankful to get away from him.

She found herself working with John Pollock, which made things easier and after three nerve-racking hours, when it seemed as if the young woman on the operating table couldn't possibly survive her injuries, they finished and she was wheeled off to the ward.

'She'd better have another three pints of blood,' John said wearily. 'Will you see to it, Jean?'

By the time she had finished coping with the new admissions and done a quick round of the old patients, it was nearly two in the morning. She trailed into the residents' quarters, too drained of energy for any thought. The lights were still on in the Mess. She glanced in and stiffened as she saw Pollock and his wife having a drink with Alex.

'Come and join us,' Pollock called. 'You could do with a nightcap, judging by your appearance.'

She dropped into a chair, took the drink he poured for her, and sipped it with her eyes shut. The others were talking about the beauty of the Lake District, which Alex seemed to know well.

'Your boys will love living on the edge of it. A good place to bring up a family.'

Jean looked up, found him watching her steadily, with

slightly puckered eyebrows, and looked down again quickly. She drained her glass and rose. 'I'm all in. Please excuse me.'

She was halfway to the door when Nancy Pollock spoke. 'Perhaps you'll look us up some day if you're ever in the North. We haven't an address yet, of course.'

'Doctors are easy to find through the Medical Directory,' her husband pointed out.

'Of course.' Politeness demanded that she come back and make them a proper farewell. She got out a few stilted words and turned stiffly to Alex.

'I'll say goodbye to you too, Mr Mackenzie. I don't suppose I'll see you in the morning.'

It was like a scene in a play, not something that was happening to her. She held out her hand and he took it in his.

'What formality, Jean!' A quick smile came and went. He gave her a close look. 'You're out on your feet, my dear girl. Off to bed with you. At least you can have a lie in tomorrow. Come and see me in my office before you go, please. Soon after midday.'

Dismayed, she stared at him. There was nothing he could say, however well intended, that would make her feel any better.

'I'm sorry,' she said, her voice a little hoarse, 'but I want to be off as early as possible.'

He was still holding her hand and she tugged it away. 'I can't wait to leave,' she said breathlessly. 'Goodbye.'

Jean caught a look of surprise on Nancy Pollock's face, the quick glance exchanged between Pollock and Alex, and as she started up the stairs to her room Alex said something which she couldn't catch. What had it been?

'Good riddance! She always was an awkward girl.' She would never know now.

Later, lying sleepless in the dark, she wished she hadn't been so ungracious, that she had managed some polite platitude instead of that truthful but tactless remark. For she was glad to be leaving Westhampton, and she would never come back. If Tony or Peter or any of her other friends wanted to see her, they would have to come to London to do so.

She hadn't had time to pack on Thursday, and on Friday morning she was late up. She had a quick cup of coffee and then got down to the task of sorting out her belongings. Astonishing what a lot of junk one collected in a year! It took her longer than she expected and it was nearly twelve before she snapped the last of her cases shut.

She was desperate to get away before Alex finished in the fracture clinic, because the thought of meeting him again was too painful to contemplate. She lugged her two heaviest cases down to the car and went back for the rest. She had a last look round to make sure she had left nothing behind, ran a comb through her hair and turned when she heard a footstep on the landing.

Alex stood in the doorway, a little half smile on his face, as if he wasn't quite sure of his welcome.

'You were going to leave without coming to see me,' he said quietly, 'weren't you, Jean?'

There was a curious roaring sound in her ears and she felt as if she was going to faint. 'Please go away,' she whispered. 'Please! You can't possibly have anything to say.'

For answer he shut the door and walked towards her. 'You're right, little one. I haven't anything to say.'

He pulled her into his arms and his mouth came down on hers. He pressed her body against his and kissed her again, and when he released her he was breathing as fast as she was.

'I've wanted to do that for a long time,' he murmured. 'Four months, to be exact. Jean, tell me I didn't imagine what I saw in your eyes last night. That you do care?'

She was still confused and uncertain. 'If you're just trying to be kind——'

'Kind!' he exploded. 'I've told you before that my feelings towards you aren't in the least kind. You've driven me nearly crazy, my love. You're the only girl I've ever lost any sleep over. Does that convince you? Can't you believe that I want to marry you?'

The future that had seemed so bleak was suddenly full of joy. 'Oh, Alex!' she sighed, and went into his arms again. A long time later she said dreamily, 'It's a pity I have to go home.'

He held her away from him. 'Why do you have to go? I'm off this weekend. Come to the cottage with me and meet my sister and her family. They're arriving this evening.'

'Will there be enough room?'

'I can sleep on the sofa. Ring your family, Jean. And you can tell them you've just got engaged.'

She gave him a loving but slightly mischievous look. 'Aren't you assuming a lot? Did I say yes?'

Her mother answered the telephone and listened calmly to her daughter's news. 'Well, thank goodness for that, darling! I hope you'll be more like your old self now. And when are we going to see your Alex? Tom speaks very highly of him.' Being Mrs Muir she added a crisp comment that she hoped Alex wasn't one of those men who objected to a working wife. Such a waste of all that training, if a girl gave up when she married.

So Jean promised that she would bring Alex home on Sunday. In the car on the way to the cottage she asked him if he would mind her working part time.

'Of course not. You're a good doctor, sweetheart, and I'll be proud to have a wife who's as smart as she's pretty.'

They had halted at a crossroads and he gave her a quick frowning glance. 'I suppose I'm getting the best of the bargain. I know I'm not the easiest man in the world to get on with. But I love you very much, Jean, and if there's one thing I've learnt it's that success means nothing—nothing at all—without the right person to share it with.'

From a loner like Alex that was quite an admission. Jean gave his hand a quick squeeze.

'I used to think it was Pauline you wanted to marry. Didn't you once?'

He changed into first gear before speaking.

'No post-mortems on my past girl-friends, please, and I won't drag up Tony! No, I never even thought of marrying her. I suppose I used to go around with girls like Pauline because I didn't want to get too involved. Not until I met you, anyway.'

When they reached the cottage Alex said cheerfully, 'We've an hour or two on our own, before my sister and her family arrive. Let's make the most of it!'

She went happily into his arms, but they had scarcely exchanged one kiss before a shrill voice came from behind them.

'Hallo, Mr Mackenzie! We didn't know you were coming.'

Alex let her go with a muttered curse, and turned to Simon and his brother.

'Belt off, you two! Haven't you any tact at all? Jean and I have just decided to get married.'

Their grubby faces were split by approving grins. 'Golly, that's great! Then you'll be celebrating.' Simon stumbled over the big word. 'So we'll have to stay. You know, to drink your health. I love beer!'

Alex gave an expressive shrug. 'It's no good, sweetheart, we've company whether we want it or not. You sit out here and I'll fetch the drinks. Bitter lemon for you two,' he added with a ferocious glare.

Giggling, they skipped into the house with him, and Jean sat down on the stone seat. Hearing their happy voices through the open door, she thought how good Alex was with children, how good he would be with his own children.

She remembered her disappointment when the boys had turned up, on that last visit to the cottage. This time it didn't matter, because she would have Alex's company for the rest of her life.

When they rejoined her Alex handed her a sherry and raised his own glass.

'Here's to us, Jean. Wish us luck, boys.'

'You won't need luck,' Simon said very seriously, 'because she's so nice.'

Alex smiled down at them, his dark face full of warmth. 'How right you are, Simon! Now drink up, my love, because as usual the boys are hungry and are waiting to be fed.'

# Doctor Nurse Romances

# Romance in modern medical life

Read more about the lives and loves of doctors and nurses in the fascinatingly different backgrounds of contemporary medicine. These are the four Doctor Nurse romances to look out for next month.

**SURGEON'S CHOICE**
Hazel Fisher

**NURSE AT TWIN VALLEYS**
Lilian Darcy

**DOCTOR'S DIAGNOSIS**
Grace Read

**THE END OF THE RAINBOW**
Betty Neels

Buy them from your usual paperback stockist, or write to: Mills & Boon Reader Service, P.O. Box 236, Thornton Rd, Croydon, Surrey CR9 3RU, England. Readers in South Africa-write to: Mills & Boon Reader Service of Southern Africa, Private Bag X3010, Randburg, 2125.

**Mills & Boon**

the rose of romance

# Doctor Nurse Romances

Amongst the intense emotional pressures of modern medical life, doctors and nurses often find romance. Read about their lives and loves in the other three Doctor Nurse titles available this month.

**SURGEON ON SKORA**
*by Lynne Collins*
Theatre Nurse Judith Henty and surgeon Brad Hamilton make a splendid surgical team. What does it matter that outside the operating theatre they simply can't get on?

**NOT AGAIN, NURSE!**
*by Leonie Craig*
Emma Benedict wants to be a really good nurse, a modern-day Florence Nightingale, but somehow all she does results in chaos. And when she comes into contact with Senior Registrar Garrard Blair life becomes almost unbearable...

**THE CRY OF THE SWAN**
*by Sarah Franklin*
Nicola Page is keen to get the job as Staff Nurse at the Meadowlands Rehabilitation Centre until she finds that Simon Grey — who belongs firmly in her past — is on the board of interviewers. If she accepts the job will she once more be running headlong into heartache?

**Mills & Boon**
the rose of romance

# A very special gift for Mother's Day

You love Mills & Boon romances. Your mother will love this attractive Mother's Day gift pack. First time in paperback, four superb romances by leading authors. A very special gift for Mother's Day.

United Kingdom £4.40

On sale from 24th Feb 1984

**A Grand Illusion**
Maura McGiveny

**Desire in the Desert**
Mary Lyons

**Sensual Encounter**
Carole Mortimer

**Aquamarine**
Madeleine Ker

Look for this gift pack where you buy Mills & Boon romances.

# 4 BOOKS FREE

## Enjoy a Wonderful World of Romance...

Passionate and intriguing, sensual and exciting. A top quality selection of four Mills & Boon titles written by leading authors of Romantic fiction can be delivered direct to your door absolutely FREE!

Try these Four Free books as your introduction to Mills & Boon Reader Service. You can be among the thousands of women who enjoy six brand new Romances every month PLUS a whole range of special benefits.

- Personal membership card.
- Free monthly newsletter packed with recipes, competitions, exclusive book offers and a monthly guide to the stars.
- Plus extra bargain offers and big cash savings.

There is no commitment whatsoever, no hidden extra charges and your first parcel of four books is absolutely FREE!

Why not send for more details now? Simply complete and send the coupon to MILLS & BOON READER SERVICE, P.O. BOX 236, THORNTON ROAD, CROYDON, SURREY, CR9 3RU, ENGLAND. OR why not telephone us on 01-684 2141 and we will send you details about the Mills & Boon Reader Service Subscription Scheme – you'll soon be able to join us in a wonderful world of Romance.

Please note:– READERS IN SOUTH AFRICA write to Mills & Boon Ltd., Postbag X3010, Randburg 2125, S. Africa.

Please send me details of the Mills & Boon Reader Service Subscription Scheme.

NAME (Mrs/Miss) ______________________ EP6

ADDRESS ______________________

______________________

COUNTY/COUNTRY ______________________

POSTCODE ______________________

BLOCK LETTERS PLEASE